When Dreams Collide

by John Mark LeMaster

This is a work of fiction. The events and characters described herein are imaginary and are not intended to refer to specific places or living persons. The opinions expressed in this manuscript are solely the opinions of the author and do not represent the opinions or thoughts of the publisher. The author has represented and warranted full ownership and/or legal right to publish all the materials in this book.

When Dreams Collide
All Rights Reserved.
Copyright © 2013 John Mark LeMaster
v3.0

Cover Illustration by Katina Vicari. All rights reserved - used with permission.

Scriptures taken from the Holy Bible, New International Version®, NIV®. Copyright © 1973, 1978, 1984, 2011 by Biblica, Inc.™ Used by permission of Zondervan. All rights reserved worldwide. www.zondervan.com The "NIV" and "New International Version" are trademarks registered in the United States Patent and Trademark Office by Biblica, Inc.™"

This book may not be reproduced, transmitted, or stored in whole or in part by any means, including graphic, electronic, or mechanical without the express written consent of the publisher except in the case of brief quotations embodied in critical articles and reviews.

Outskirts Press, Inc.
http://www.outskirtspress.com

ISBN: 978-1-4787-1951-9

Outskirts Press and the "OP" logo are trademarks belonging to Outskirts Press, Inc.

PRINTED IN THE UNITED STATES OF AMERICA

Acknowledgements

First, I want to acknowledge the Lord Jesus Christ who changed me from the inside out and made me into a different person. This book was birthed from the heart of God and I hope and pray I am able to convey what He has shown me. His grace, mercy, and love have never failed to amaze me in so many ways.

I want to thank my best friend, Dean Cartin. He has been such a faithful friend and encouragement to me during one of the darkest times in my life. He is one of greatest prayer warriors I have ever seen and I hope to emulate his ever enduring zeal for God.

I want to thank my mom, Charlotte, who was probably one of the greatest moms I could ever ask for. In every way, she was a giver. It consumed her as love poured from her to me and others. I was with her as she entered heaven and hope to imitate the incredible life she lived.

I want to thank my dad, John Allen. I remember as a child, my dad worshipping the Lord at the top of his lungs as tears poured down his face. I have been deeply enriched by having a great relationship with him throughout the years.

I want to thank my children for being such an awesome blessing for me; Clark, Caleb, and Carson. Each with such a different personality, talented, intelligent, humorous, and best of all, lovers of God.

I want to acknowledge Christina and Cory. They both died from miscarriages before I knew them. I had a dream one night. Two children were bouncing on a bed and were having a great time. I was trying to tell them to stop but I didn't know their names. My son Carson was in the dream and became angry with me for forgetting their names. I asked him their names and he said "Christina and Cory". I knew they were my children because I always name my children with the letter C. The dream was telling me to never forget them. I know they will be in heaven to greet me. I can't wait to see them again. You will see their impact on this book.

I want to thank the editors of this book, Amanda Morris and Jim Bryson. Considering how bad my English skills are, they pulled off a miracle to get this book in its present form.

I want to thank Katina Vicari for the cover design. Blessings for you.

I want to thank Dr. Mark Virkler for his book, *How to Hear the Voice of God*. His book helped this chronic left-brained engineer to open up to God in a new way. This book was birthed in one of those listening/looking sessions. Once the vision got started, I couldn't shut it down until this book was finished (nine years later).

I want to thank all of my friends at the Life Center in Aiken, South Carolina. They were always encouraging me on my book.

I want to thank my family (my two brothers, step dad, nieces, etc.) for being so good to me.

The list of others in my life is endless and I acknowledge their positive input in my life.

Chapter 1
The Angel

Listening to the laughter filling the playground, an enormous heavenly being towered above two children. He reached down to steady the top of the swing set rocking from the energetic youngsters. This fourteen-foot tall angel had just received the assignment that would usher in the destiny of nations. The formulated plan was unveiling, for Heaven was invading Earth and the first of the generals was arriving.

The forces of wickedness felt the angel's presence in the region but could not pinpoint his exact location. The demons of darkness hissed and growled as they felt his arrival. In their arrogance, they opened a door for their defenses to be penetrated.

An autumn wind blew through Sharpsville, a small town in rural Kentucky. The city stood away from the outside world, its isolation providing cover. Two young children played, unaware of the unfolding destiny that would alter the entire world with a tsunami of heavenly change.

"Hey, TJ watch this," said Charlie Harris as he leapt from the swing and landed on the spread of woodchips. His dark skin and handsome features accented his contagious smile. His friend, Tom Johnson, leapt off as the swing reached the height of the arc, copying Charlie's daring jump. Landing successfully farther in the woodchips, he laughed and ran back to the swing to try it again as the sweat dripped off his brown curls and onto his dimpled chin. The striking difference in their appearances didn't seem to influence their opinion of each other. They were best of friends.

The angel smiled as he marveled at the genius of God's plan. He turned to face one of his captains as they arrived.

"Commander Trojol, we must go to the hill. We will have only a few minutes to launch the operation before the enemy comes," the captain told him.

"Let's go," Trojol said as the two instantly translated to the war hill. Trojol stood at the top of the crest overlooking the Kentucky countryside. The lush valley was filled with small farmhouses and productive fields of corn and soybeans. As a table was placed before him, Trojol rolled out a large scroll containing the plans.

As he memorized the details, hundreds of shafts of light were descending from heaven to the valley below. As each shaft struck the earth, the ground shook and a burst of light exploded.

Feeling a darkness coming, he rolled up the scroll and handed it to the captain. "The Lord bless you on your assignment," Trojol said as the other angels disappeared.

Within seconds, a large hideous creature of tremendous strength appeared.

"The great Trojol," spoke the hideous demon. "We meet again. Your invasion plans are doomed to fail because these chosen ones are too weak. Our army can destroy them easily. Your boss is a fool for depending on these children. I'll kill them before they ever become men. Or perhaps I'll keep them alive but destroy their souls. Not even you will want them."

"Apollyon, you will never defeat God's plan for these two. I will see to that," Trojol answered.

"They are mere men, they will fall," Apollyon said as he disappeared, leaving behind his stench.

Trojol smiled. He was built for war, and the battles he had dreamed of were taking shape.

Two years later, Tom tapped on a weathered wooden door. A tall slender African-American woman answered, "Tom, come right in. Charlie's in his room. I'll get him."

As Charlie bounded down the stairs, he greeted his friend. "Hey, Tom, What's up?" Charlie asked. Tom stammered for an answer as he fidgeted. Charlie had never seen his friend act like this before.

"What's the matter?" Charlie asked.

"Well, I'm moving and I probably won't get to see you very much. I'm going with my Mom to Creighton. She found a job there. My Dad is staying here,"

"Why can't you stay with your dad?" Charlie asked.

"Well, they're divorcing and the judge says I have to go with my mom," Tom said as he looked at the floor. "I'll come back when I can to visit you,"

"OK. Are we still gonna be friends?" Charlie asked.

"Yeah, we'll always be friends," Tom assured him. Then he waved goodbye and walked away as Charlie waved back.

As Tom rode in the car, he finished his drawing of the swing he left behind in Sharpsville. He retraced the lines and added details so he could remember the good times with Charlie. He remained very quiet throughout the trip. After the divorce, Tom changed from the happy child he once was. His mom, Cheryl Johnson, tried but failed in getting him to open up.

"We're here," she said brightly as they pulled into the unfamiliar driveway. Tom continued to look at his drawing to see if there was anything to add.

"I know it's hard moving to a new area but you can make new friends," she said.

Her words provided no comfort, only adding to the awkward pain that Tom felt. After repeated requests, he emerged from the car to see a much smaller house. He dragged into the house and walked through each room. His silence spoke volumes about his feelings for the new house. He found the nearest couch and laid down for a long nap.

For months, Tom continued in his isolation. He remained quiet and distant at school as well as at home. One Sunday, his mom surprised him. "Get up, we are going to church today," she demanded.

"I don't want to go. We never went to church in Sharpsville," Tom protested.

"It won't hurt you. Get ready," she repeated.

Her persistence paid off; Tom got dressed. As they pulled into the parking lot, Tom peeked out the window to see a large clapboard building on the edge of town, bordered by hardwoods and fields. His mom bounded out of the car as Tom crawled out the other side. She insisted on walking in together.

As she opened the front door, all eyes turned to them. Tom bristled at their stares and knew something was wrong. He could see the smiles were forced, the greetings were reserved, and the pastor seemed overeager to meet them.

Tom and his mom sat down as the service started promptly on time. Everything seemed to run on a schedule. The pastor even got angry on cue. Tom began to squirm in his seat.

"Stop that," his mom whispered.

Tom couldn't stop. His skin itched, the seat felt hard, and soon, the pastor was glaring at him.

I've got a bad feeling about this, Tom thought.

The sermon ended precisely on time, and Tom felt a wave of relief as he bolted for the car. He was glad it was over.

After everyone left the church, the pastor locked the building. He didn't notice the hideous creature sitting in the chair behind the pulpit. "I think I'm going to enjoy going to church here," said Apollyon as his hairy red skin rubbed the podium.

To Tom's surprise, his mom continued to go to the church. He fought with her but she seemed dead set on going. His mom would also call the church for help from time to time. This made Tom all the more resistant.

After one service, Tom noticed the pastor and his mom having a long talk behind the church. Since it was in a secluded spot and the pastor was married, Tom felt evil chills down his spine. Soon, every time he looked around, his mom and the pastor were staring at each other. Tom hated the church so much that he spent his time seeking a hiding place. Most of the time a small janitor's closet did the trick.

One day as he sat in his hiding place, he overheard a conversation in the women's restroom.

"The pastor and the new lady Cheryl are making eyes at each other again," one woman said.

"I wonder how his wife Edith puts up with that behavior," another woman replied.

"You know Edith and Pastor Gill have never gotten along with each other. I heard Edith has threatened to leave him over his flirting. Don't tell anyone that we talked about this. The pastor will kick us out of the choir for spreading rumors like he did to Elizabeth," the first woman said.

"I think his middle initial T stands for Tyrant," the other woman said as they both giggled.

Although Tom agreed with the comment, he did not laugh. He realized his misgivings about Pastor Gill were true. From then on, he found a new determination in his fight to avoid church, but for his mother, it was already too late. The hook was firmly lodged in her jaw.

Within a number of weeks, Pastor Gill had to travel out of town for a minister's conference. There was a visiting minister preaching while he was gone. Tom seemed to enjoy him much more. His mom felt encouraged at her son's new interest in church.

After the service, Tom felt tired and fell fast asleep on the living room couch. He slipped into a dream where He was walking down a country road. It seemed to be similar to the Creighton area but he couldn't recall where it was. He walked towards a distant bridge. Everything seemed so real. He could hear the birds singing and smell the flowers.

As Tom approached the bridge, he squinted to see a couple on the edge of the bridge. They were fighting.

Tom ran to see who it was but stopped abruptly when he recognized the couple. It was Pastor Gill and his wife Edith.

"Who is she, Gill? How many has it been?" Edith yelled.

"Would you just shut up? If you were half the wife I needed, this would never have to happen," Gill replied.

"No, I won't shut up. I'm going to let everyone know.

It's about time they all knew anyway," Edith replied.

Gill grabbed his wife and dragged her to the guard railing. She fought until her strength gave out. Then she froze when she saw the creature. A large demon stood behind Gill. It was three feet taller than a normal man. As it extended its wings, it seemed to give Gill supernatural strength.

Gill seized the chance and threw Edith over the guard rail. Her wedding ring caught on the railing and kept her from falling into the icy waters below.

"Gill, I can't swim," she cried out.

"It's too late, Edith," he said as he stomped her hand with his muddy boot. She plunged towards the creek below, struck the rocks and fell unconscious. She slipped under the water and never resurfaced.

"Are you sure no one will suspect me?" Gill said to the demon Apollyon.

"If you hold my hands, I will transport you back to the seminar in Kansas City," Apollyon promised.

Gill smiled as he grabbed the creature's hands, which were like the talons of an eagle. Tom gasped and started to run away. Gill and Apollyon both turned to see him and started to chase him. Tom felt his strength leave as the demon closed in on him. He felt the beast's breath on his neck a moment before he was transported back to his living room in Creighton. It was just a dream.

Tom sat up, his heart racing. He ran to his mom's room.

"Momma, I had a bad dream," he said.

"What were you dreaming about?" She asked as she hugged him.

"I was being chased by a demon and … ahhh … Where is Pastor Gill?" he asked.

"He's at a minister's conference in Kansas City. Do you want to talk to him?" She asked.

"No, Where's his wife?" he asked.

"Do you want me to check on Edith?" she asked.

"Yes, can you call her?" he asked.

"Ok, I'll get the phone," she replied.

His mom picked up the phone and dialed her number. Edith didn't answer. This was unusual. Cheryl called a neighbor to check on her.

It's odd that she didn't go to the seminar and she didn't go to church this morning, Cheryl thought to herself.

The neighbor told Cheryl that Edith wasn't home and that her car had been gone since yesterday. Since Edith had been gone for twenty four hours, the neighbor called the police. Word quickly spread, and the whole town gathered to look for her.

Three days into the search, Tom told a policeman about his dream involving Edith and the bridge, leaving out the details of Gill's involvement. The police knew of five such creeks in the area. On one of the bridges, they found blood belonging to Edith. Then they found her body in the creek below and ruled it a homicide due to her mangled hand and missing wedding ring.

Finding her body so quickly only solidified Gill's alibi that he was in Kansas City at the time of the murder.

He was removed from the suspect list.

At the funeral, Tom tried to stay hidden as much as possible. A large crowd from the community showed up and paid their last respects. Every time Tom saw Gill, he fought to not gasp. He knew he couldn't go to the police because his story was not believable. But for Tom, the images were still fresh in his mind.

Gill spoke at the funeral and showed a gratuitous amount of sorrow, enough to draw sympathy and divert the naysayers. Edith was buried in a closed casket at Gill's request.

Tom began acting out whenever his mother was around, yet his actions produced the wrong effect. She started spending more time with Gill to "comfort" him. She even began extensive counseling sessions with him. The more Tom tried to fight it, the more she seemed to fall in love with Gill.

Soon, Gill was showing up at their house for dinner. Tom never left his room, and remained even more reserved.

He retreated into a world of heavy metal music and violent video games. His descent worried his mom and she suggested he get counseling from Gill. Tom's response scared her.

"I would rather die that talk to him," Tom stammered. Tom was deathly scared of this man but he could not tell anyone why.

His mom continued her efforts to "help" Tom, yet she was falling hard for her new man, Pastor Gill. He was everything she wanted in a man, or so she thought.

Within a month, she sat Tom down and told him the dreaded news. "Tom, Gill and I are getting married. I have thought about this a lot and I need someone in my life right now. I know he's not perfect but he'll make a good stepdad for you. It's our opportunity to be a family again."

Tom didn't utter a word. He saw this day coming. He went straight to his room, slammed the door, and turned up his music. He searched through one of his drawers looking for a CD. He found a picture of him and Charlie at the playground in Sharpsville. He smiled when he thought about those long days in the sun, swinging and laughing for hours. He laid on his bed and went into a powerful dream.

He was on the playground with Charlie, jumping from the swing. As he landed, he felt himself falling backwards. Without warning, he felt a large hand stopping his fall. He turned and gazed at a large angel dressed in white with a golden sash.

"I am sent to make sure you don't fall. You are abundantly blessed by the Father above. His love surrounds your every step," the angel said to him.

A gentle breeze began to blow across Tom's face.

The dream ended and Tom awoke to a clear, sunny day. He felt peace again, and it seemed foreign to him. He got up and greeted his mom for breakfast. She smiled, thinking that Tom had come to terms with the wedding.

Chapter 2
Charlie Harris

Charlie lived with his mom, Emma Harris, in a small house in Sharpsville. He looked at the playground where he and Tom played. He was a bright and energetic youngster but he was tired today. He began his walk home, wondering what his mom was making for dinner. He became distracted by a caterpillar.

"I almost stepped on you, boy. I'll move you to a safe place where no one will hurt you," he said to the insect. He stared and smiled at it to see if it noticed him. Charlie loved life and noticed every sunset. Although he seemed ordinary, he had an extraordinary call of God on his life.

He loved church and went as often as he could. He loved to sing the songs that he learned there. He sang most any time, day or night. He always felt God's presence as he sang. His mother always smiled when she heard his little voice belting out tunes of joy.

Although Charlie had a simple and joyful life, his mom struggled to make ends meet. So Charlie didn't have many of the things that the other kids had. It didn't seem to bother him, but it bothered his mother. Charlie's faith was strong. He reasoned if he needed something, he could pray for it and God would give it to him. More than once, Charlie's prayer of faith helped pull the family through.

Charlie's mom closed her eyes one night and tried to stop the thoughts about her ex-husband Jim, Charlie's dad. For her, it was too painful. She didn't want to tell Charlie about his brutality and cruelty. Jim only thought of himself and how he was affected by things. She thought a child would help their relationship but it just made things worse. She didn't want Charlie to know his father was in prison.

Yet the big secret she held was the reason he was imprisoned. He had tried to kill her. She could still see him on the night it all happened. Half drunk, he stole a shotgun from a friend and burst into the house.

"I'm going put an end to both of you," he screamed as she ran to the bathroom with the baby. He fired the shotgun at the door. Charlie's mom had turned her back to the door to protect the baby. The buckshot tore into her back. She thought she might die, and she prayed for the baby as she bled, but the solid wooden door had slowed the shot enough to only wound her.

With the smell of gunpowder hanging in the air, Jim fished for more shells. The neighbors heard the shot and called the police. Jim found his ammunition but cursed when he heard the sirens, and took off running. The police found him quickly, and the nightmare ended. Charlie's mom was hospitalized, but the baby was fine.

She had testified against her husband and he received 15 years for attempted 2nd degree murder. She could still see the murder in his eyes as they escorted him to prison. He would send her letters every month just to torment her, saying he was getting out soon. It worked. She lived in terror.

Many people helped his mom recover and get a job in town. She was very grateful for their help but was always fearful of Jim's return. Her thoughts continued as she took another sleeping pill, hoping she wouldn't have another sleepless night.

One night Charlie had a dream that his house was on fire. He was running through the house, trying to find his mother among the flames. As he reached the back door, a large angel stepped into the house and grabbed Charlie.

"You must come with me. I am your protector," the angel said. "You are going to a new home filled with love." Charlie reached out and touched his hand as he relaxed, feeling the wind blow through his soul. A telephone rang, and Charlie woke up.

His mom picked it up. "Ms. Harris?" a voice on the other end inquired.

"Yes, this is she."

"Ms. Harris, this Captain John Walker with the Kentucky State Police. Your ex-husband Jim Harris has just been released on parole from prison. He may want to contact you. We have alerted the Sharpsville police that he is on parole. If you see him, let them know right away, OK?"

"Thank you for the information, sir," she said softly.

"No problem, Ma'am. Good Night," he said as he hung up the phone.

As she placed the phone on the receiver, terror seized her heart. She knew what was coming but she felt powerless to stop it. She broke into tears. Charlie heard the sobbing and came into her room.

"What's the matter, mom?" Charlie asked.

"Let me hold you baby," she said as she gripped him tightly.

Outside, a car door slammed and someone banged at the front door. "Run to the neighbor's house," Charlie's mom told him.

"Why?" Charlie asked.

"There's no time to explain, just go now," she said abruptly. The person at the door started shouting. She could recognize the voice. It was Jim and she could tell that he was drunk. "Run to Nellie's house. Now go!" she said firmly. Charlie took off running out the back door and he didn't stop. Jim saw Charlie run out the back and noted his direction.

"I'll be back to get you," he muttered under his breath. He broke in the front door. "Hi honey, I'm home," he shouted. She ran into the bathroom and locked the door. "This is just like last time but you won't get a chance to testify against me. Why did you betray me?" he said. He took some gasoline and spread it outside the bathroom door.

"I'll be here when you are ready to come out, honey." He threw a match on the floor and ran out. The door caught fire, then spread to the walls. In another moment, the house burst into in flames as Jim laughed in the backyard. Emma prayed for her son as she breathed her last breath dying on the bathroom floor.

"It's my boy's turn now," Jim Harris said as he ran down the lane to find him, grinning with every stride. But charlie had run further than Jim realized. Charlie stopped to catch his breath and grew confused when he did not recognize where he was.

He saw a house with a good hiding spot in the back. He stayed under a bush, but the dogs across the street kept barking. Jim ran down the street and found him easily. As he approached Charlie, he said, "You thought you could get away. No one runs from me, boy."

The yard that Charlie was hiding in belonged to Beverly Parker. She noticed the strangers in her back yard and grabbed her son's old baseball bat. While Jim was yelling at Charlie, he pulled out the shotgun hidden in his coat. He tightened his grip on the weapon as he fought to get his breath. Charlie closed his eyes. Jim paused for a moment as if his conscience was finally being heard.

Jim stared at his son and, for a moment, started to feel again. Then without warning, he yielded to a sinister power as his eyes rolled back. He slowly aimed the gun at Charlie and grinned.

Jim had not heard Beverly sneaking up behind him. She instinctively swung the bat at Jim's head. Since she was an old woman, her swing should have only slightly injured him, but it did something more, surprising everyone who later heard about it. As she swung, it was as though an invisible force assisted her, giving her great power to the swing. The collision struck Jim with so much force that his neck vertebrae were instantly crushed. His head turned completely sideways. He cursed the name of God and fell to the ground in a heap. Beverly dropped the bat and screamed at the sight of him.

When the police arrived, they couldn't believe what had happened either. Charlie corroborated the story. The detectives concluded that it was self defense and were glad that the criminal had been apprehended.

Jim was still breathing but was not expected to live. He was taken to the local hospital. Charlie gave Beverly a hug and wouldn't let go.

Because there was no more family left for Charlie, social services allowed him to stay with Beverly until they could move him to a foster home. Two days later, surprising things happened. Beverly applied to be Charlie's foster parent and the application was later accepted.

Jim survived but was a quadriplegic due to his severed spinal cord. One night he suddenly rose up and escaped from his hospital room. He never appeared in Sharpsville again.

Neither did anyone want him to.

Although Beverly was 58, she found the strength and desire to raise Charlie. Charlie found a home full of love and peace. Beverly's late husband had left her enough money to provide a good life. She cared for Charlie as her own.

They went to church together. They sang together. She taught him to play piano. He always adored the piano. "Aunt Bev?" he would ask, "Will there be pianos in heaven?"

"Yes, there will most certainly be pianos in heaven." she always replied.

Beverly read him Bible stories. His favorite was David and Goliath.

"Aunt Bev, I wish I could be like King David and face Goliath. David wasn't scared of nothing or no one. I wish I was like that," Charlie said.

"You will face your Goliath and you will win, and many will be free because of you," she replied.

"Aunt Bev, I love you."

"I love you too, Charlie. I'll always be there when you need me. We are like salt and pepper. Always together," she said as she tucked him into bed.

One day, Charlie told his Aunt Bev about the dream he had before his mom died. He showed her the paper where he had written down everything. He asked her if she thought that an angel had helped her hit his dad. She sat down and said, "Oh dear." The realization hit her that she wasn't crazy but that a miracle had occurred.

The memory of the event flooded her mind. She realized that dreams can come from God, and she should pay attention to their messages. From then on, Charlie and Beverly started writing down their dreams and prayed for their interpretation. A completely new world of hearing from God opened up to them.

Beverly continued to train Charlie in the Bible. Many times at night, he was afraid of the darkness, thinking that his dad might return. Beverly had Charlie recite verses that help calm him. "Yea, though I walk through the valley of death, I will fear no evil for you are with me, (Psalms 23:3)." He repeated it until he fell asleep.

The thought of his father returning plagued Bev's mind too. She also recited verses. She formed a strong faith in the scriptures and it helped her to overcome her worries and fears. She became strong and Charlie grew under her.

One day, Charlie noticed a picture of a boy on the wall and asked who it was. "That's my son David," Beverly said proudly. "He's a missionary in Ethiopia. He's been there for 15 years now. He writes me every month or so. He says that God has moved mightily among the villagers there. He has seen tremendous miracles. But things are very dangerous. Every once in a while, their village is attacked. They pray and they are delivered. Sometimes their church gets burned to the ground and they have to rebuild it. Would you like to read his letters?" she asked.

"Yes, I'd love to," Charlie answered.

Beverly brought what looked like a hundred letters. "We can read one a night. I don't want you to lose sleep reading these letters. You have homework and chores, you know," she said. Charlie could barely hide his excitement. When most children heard a Dr. Suess book read to them every night, Charlie got a missionary letter read to him.

For some reason, Charlie's tender heart never tired of the letters. They told of struggles like learning a foreign language and culture. There was sickness and extreme poverty. Some of the people still practiced black magic, and there were many run-ins with the village witch doctor. David had learned spiritual warfare as a necessity. One day he would cast out a demon. The next day he would pray and see a healing.

The turning point for the village came when the chief went blind. The villagers thought that the witch doctor had cursed him for allowing the "white man" into their village. David fasted for three days and prayed for God's direction. On the third day, he felt he had the answer, which was to pray for the chief.

Meanwhile a crowd gathered outside David's hut to kill him when he came out. But instead of being attacked, he walked through the group and straight into the chief's hut. After David's prayer, the chief could see. The villagers stood in shock. This God was indeed more powerful than the power of the witch doctor. The villagers turned their hearts to David's message.

Night after night, Charlie read these letters. He became familiar with what to do in impossible situations. Charlie even learned the villager's customs and a few of their words.

An astonishing faith grew in Charlie. At church, Charlie helped Bev teach her Sunday school class. People were surprised at how much he knew.

Beverly Parker decided to fully adopt Charlie. The social workers were amazed at his progress. Although others were surprised at the adoption, it was no surprise to Charlie. He knew it would happen the minute he prayed for it.

Chapter 3
Tom's struggle

Tom stopped the war with his mother over Gill. The wedding was beautiful and she seemed happy. *Maybe I got it wrong about Gill. Maybe the dream doesn't mean anything,* he thought. Tom allowed himself to enjoy the wedding, feasting on cake and even catching the garter. The crowd broke out in laughter when it fell in Tom's hands and he grinned through a crimson blush.

Tom grew used to having a man in the house. He and Gill watched movies together, played baseball, and even prayed together at dinner. Tom stopped listening to his heavy-metal music and start enjoying church more.

Then one night, while Gill and Tom's mother were at a birthday party, Tom was rummaging through Gill's desk drawer looking for a pen. Instead, he found a piece of paper that caught his interest. It read: "1312 combo." The first thing that came to mind was the combination locked chest Gill had put in the attic.

Curiosity got the best of Tom, so he climbed into the attic to check out the combo. "It works," he whispered as the lock popped open. He was aware of a strange odor as he pawed through the chest, hoping to find buried treasure, but all he saw was a dirty outfit and some old boots. He flipped the boots over and gasped. Stuck to the sole was part of a human finger with a wedding ring still intact.

"Oh my God, it's true! He did kill her," he choked as the images in the dream flashed through his mind. He started to vomit, the stench of the decayed finger reaching his nostrils. *He can't know I was here,* he thought. His hands shook as he stuffed the boots back in the trunk, hastily arranging them the way he found them. He locked the trunk with a click just as he heard a car door slam in the driveway.

Gill and Tom's mother were home. Tom scrambled out of the attic and down the pull-down stairs, flipping them into the ceiling with a frantic shove, then running to his room and locking the door. Gill walked into the hall and saw the string to the attic stairs still swinging, then examined the insulation bits on the carpet below.

"Tom dear, we have some cake if you want some," his mom yelled. Tom stayed silent.

"Tom, where are you?" his mom yelled out again. Tom tousled his hair and stepped out of his room.

"Oh, there you are. Were you sleeping?" his mom asked.

"Yea, I took a nap. You back already?" he asked.

"Tom, what were you doing in the attic?" Gill asked.

"I don't go up there. It's too creepy," Tom replied. Gill stared into Tom's eyes. Tom forced himself to look away and saw the cake.

"Is that for me?" he asked.

"Yes, sweetie, have some," his mother said.

Tom took the plate as he glanced at Gill, who was staring at the attic steps string. Tom reached in his pocket and his stomach churned. The combination paper! How to put it back in the desk without being noticed? Fortunately, Gill and Tom's mother retired early, and Tom was able to slip the paper back in the desk later that night.

The next morning, Gill went into the attic to check out everything. The chest had not been moved and was still locked. When he opened it, he saw the outfit was still in its place. It struck him that, in his panic, he had completely forgotten to get rid of the evidence of his wife's murder.

"Hey honey, whatcha looking for?" Cheryl asked as she poked her head into the attic.

Hearing her voice made his heart skip.

"Don't scare me like that!" he barked, struggling to snap the chest closed before she saw its contents.

"What's your problem?" she shot back.

"Sorry, honey, I'm in a bad mood and I shouldn't take it out on you. Hey, can I make you some coffee?" Gill asked in his smoothest of voices.

"Sure, I could use a cup." She smiled uneasily, wondering what had Gill so spooked. Gill smiled too, despite his pounding heart.

"I thought you told me no one would suspect me. Now my stepson is snooping around. You broke your promise," Gill shouted at the demon Apollyon.

"Shut up, idiot. I can kill you in a second. I did what I said. I transported you five-hundred miles to provide you with an alibi. You are the idiot for not burning the evidence. Tom knows what you did because I saw him in the attic. He is a great liar. There is one way to fix this. I will tempt Tom to attack you, and you can kill him in self-defense," Apollyon said.

"I'm tired of killing. Tom doesn't deserve this. He's a decent kid," Gill said wearily.

"It's too late for guilt, fool. This is your only way out. Or you can die in jail. It's up to you." said Apollyon with a flourish of his sulfur-tinged wings.

"Were you in the attic?" Gill asked Tom later that day.

"No," Tom answered.

"Don't lie to me!" Gill yelled back.

"I wasn't in the creepy attic," Tom retorted.

"Gill, what's the matter?" Cheryl asked.

"Your son is lying to us. The door to the attic had been opened and I saw his footprints in the dust," Gill said.

"Well, it's his house too, if he wants to look in the attic, what's the problem?"

"Cheryl, the problem is he is lying to us and needs to be punished. The attic is dangerous and he could get hurt or break something," Gill insisted.

Tom knew his cover was blown, so he tried a different strategy.

"I'm sorry for lying. I was just looking for an old toy. I won't go in 'your' attic again," Tom said, glancing at his mother as he emphasized "your."

"I need some alone time with Tom," Gill said to Cheryl.

Tom knew what that meant, and took off running. Gill caught up with him in the backyard, knocked him down and began flailing his writhing body with a leather belt. "If you ever tell anyone, I will break every bone in your body and I will kill your mother. Is that what you want? You want her dead?" hissed a breathless Gill.

"No," Tom cried, grimacing from the pain as blood soaked his shirt and pants.

The next day, Tom laid in his bed and yelled through his locked door that he was too sick for school. His mom couldn't understand the sudden change in Tom or Gill. Tom slept all day while Gill worked at the church. In the afternoon, Cheryl finally went to her son's door and insisted he unlock it. She gasped as she saw the blood in his clothes.

"I'm going to break his freaking neck for this," she muttered, shaking with rage as she cleansed and bandaged Tom's wounds.

"Don't, mom, you don't know what kind of man he is," Tom pleaded.

"We'll just have to find out," she said as she grabbed her car keys, her face reddened.

She drove down to the church and burst into his office. "What did you do to Tom?"

"He tripped and fell when he was running from me last night. He refused to go to the doctor. I'm trying to let him make some choices for himself." Gill answered.

"Those aren't marks from falling. Who do think you are to beat my son like that?" Cheryl yelled.

Gill slowly walked up to Cheryl and slapped her so hard that she almost passed out. "How dare you question my judgment? The boy is weak and a liar. I'm the man of the house. You will submit to me. Apologize now, or you and your son are on your own."

Cheryl trembled in fear for her and her son. She did not see this coming. She cowered and offered a barely audible apology as Gill smiled grimly.

It took six months for Tom to get the courage to escape. He took Gill's blood soaked boots from the chest as collateral, and packed his own clothes with shaking hands. He knew a few neighbors who could help him call his father to pick him up.

As Tom sneaked downstairs, he heard Gill working on the kitchen sink. It was always clogged. Tom had brought his pen knife and held it behind him, just in case. He was almost out the front door when his suitcase bumped the frame.

"Who's there?" Gill called from under the sink.

Tom remained silent. Gill poked his head out to see the shadow of the suitcase in the hallway. Tom made a mad dash from the house. Gill chased him through the door and into the street. Tom ran swiftly but the suitcase was heavy. He ran until his breath gave out, then Gill tackled him. In desperation, Tom plunged the knife into Gill's shoulder. Gill yelled and grabbed at the knife while Tom struggled to his feet. Gill pulled the knife from the bleeding wound, continued chasing Tom and caught him a few blocks down the road. This time, Gill had the knife in hand and murder on his mind. Tom cried out as Gill wrestled him to the ground, raised the knife, and started to plunge it in him. Tom closed his eyes and waited for the pain.

But the pain never came. Gill's rage turned to shock and then disbelief as a large hand held back Gill's arm. The angel then pulled Gill upright until they were eye to eye, Gill's feet dangling several feet off the ground.

"Do not touch the boy, for he is chosen!" Trojol said, tossing Gill's quaking body into a large oak tree. Tom could hear Gill's ribs breaking as he struck the trunk.

Cheryl, who had heard Tom bolt from the house, came running and found them both lying near the road. Gill explained through his pain that he tried to stop Tom from running away, and that Tom had tried to kill him. Cheryl saw Gill's knife wound and looked questionably at her son. At Gill's insistence, Tom was arrested for attempted murder. With his mother sobbing in the courtroom, Tom was convicted on assault and battery charges, and sentenced to three years in the local juvenile detention center.

Cheryl disappeared a few months later and was never seen again. Gill had an alibi and was cleared of any suspicion. He later remarried. Tom grieved for his mother—suspecting the truth and knowing he could never returned to the town of Creighton.

Bryce Johnson brought his Lexus to a stop outside the detention center. He paused as he put the car in park and sighed deeply.

"I don't feel very good about this," said his wife, Lacy, seated beside him.

"I don't have any choice in the matter. He's my son and nobody can find his mom. Besides, he'll be eighteen in a few years and then he won't be our problem anymore," said Bryce as he unbuckled the seat belt. Lacy stared straight ahead.

"I'll be back in a few minutes," Bryce said to his young bride. As he walked heavily into the juvenile detention center, he thought of everything he had to do at the office. Success came at a cost. His work helped him escape the guilt of losing his first family; now he was getting a piece of it back, he hoped.

He approached the desk.

"I'm here for Tom Johnson."

The clerk looked up. "And you are…?"

"His father."

After a few minutes, the heavy security door buzzed and Tom came through, escorted by two guards. Bryce gasped at the sight of his son. Tom looked at his dad through his swollen eyes, red from years of sleep deprivation. "The car is this way," Bryce muttered, not knowing what else to say.

"Hey, bud, you're going home," his dad said as they walked toward the car.

Tom wasn't sure what "home" meant anymore, but he climbed in the back of the car.

"Tom, this is my wife. Uh, I guess that means she's your stepmom," his dad said.

"You can call me 'Lacy'," she said as she reached out

her hand. Tom ignored her hand and stared out the window. Lacy looked at her husband with concern. Tom remained silent the entire way home. Invisible to all, the demon Apollyon rode in the back seat, grinning with sinister delight.

"Hell's plan is working just fine," he said.

Tom settled into his new life as best he could. The juvenile detention center had done a crude but effective job of hardening his emotions. He hung out with the rougher crowd at school. They were the only ones who accepted him for the mess he was. His school work suffered from his lack of sleep, yet he was still able to pass all of his classes.

Tom argued with his step-mom most of the time. One night while his dad was travelling and Tom was listening to music in his room, a car pulled in the driveway and left quickly. Tom came down the stairs to investigate and couldn't find Lacy anywhere. Three hours later, Lacy reappeared as a car outside sped away. After that, Tom paid closer attention and noticed that she disappeared a lot when his father was out of town.

One night, after getting his driver's license, Tom followed Lacy. His heart pounded as he tried to stay out of sight. He finally saw what he suspected.

In the motel room, Lacy's boyfriend turned from the window and closed the blind.

"I think your step-son saw us," said he said nervously.

"How? What? WHEN! What's he doing snooping around?" cried Lacy. "What do we do now? Oh God! I guess I could deny it. It worked before." She started to pace the floor.

"I have a plan. Didn't you say he has trouble sleeping? Maybe we could give him something and get him so hooked, he would never cross us."

"We'd have to move quick," said Lacy.

"Oxycodone ought to do the trick," he said as a smile broke out over his face.

"Awesome," she replied, and reached for his arms.

WHEN DREAMS COLLIDE

Two days later, Tom was lying on his bed, staring at the ceiling.
"Tom, can I come in?" Lacy said.
"Sure," he said.
"Tom, I got the doctor to prescribe something so you can sleep at night," she replied.
"When did you ever care about me or my sleep?" he shot back.
"Do you want to sleep or not?" she asked.
"Alright fine, give 'em here," Tom said as he swallowed the pills angrily. That night, he slept for 10 hours. It was the best night's sleep he had had in years. He loved it.

It wasn't long before He was hooked and making a deal with Lacy. She'd get him anything he wanted as long as he kept quiet about her affair.

Tom's dad suspected nothing, but noticed changes in his son. The peace in the house was wonderful. He figured everything was fine. He was never more wrong in his life.

As Tom injected the heroin into his veins, he rolled his eyes and threw his head back. "This is awesome. I could live with this feeling forever," he said as the pleasure consumed his body.

His chemical bliss was interrupted by the phone. It was his friends inviting him to go to an amusement park. Tom knew they only invited him because he was their source, but he didn't care. The park was an hour away and the partying would be intense. A smile broke out over his face as he answered, "Yea, OK dude, let's go!"

At the park, the combination of drugs in Tom's system created a very bad high for him. As darkness covered the park, the group elected to ride the killer coaster with its double-backward flips. Tom bragged about how many times he had taken on the coaster. But as he took his seat, he reached for the roll bar and couldn't feel his grip. He tried touching his hands together but couldn't feel those either. As his panicked mind started to race, his friends laughed at the worried look in his eyes.

"What's the matter, tough guy? Afraid of a little ride?"

He started to scream for them to stop the ride as the seats thrust forward, but it was too late. He struggled for every breath as his friends ignored his increasing panic. He closed his eyes, only to see images of himself falling from the seat and crashing on the ground below. He forced his eyes open to remind himself that he was still harnessed into the seat as the next backward loop rushed toward him.

He gasped as his stomach fell. The coaster raced into the next flip as Tom labored to breathe. He resisted the vertigo and finally caught his breath as the ride ended. He scrambled from his seat to vomit in a place less obvious.

"Dude, you need to chill," one friend said.

"I guess we can't take you anywhere," another added.

"It's not funny. I'm sick, dude. Take me home. NOW!"

"I guess you need your mommy," one kid snickered.

"Shut your face, you jerk. Let's go," Tom said.

His friends cursed under their breath as they made their way to the car. On the way home, the teens remained subdued, tension rising, on the verge of a fight, but they managed to maintain their cool. Tom sat in the passenger seat with his head slumped forward. Kyle, who was the least stoned, drove carefully. Tom relaxed and soon nodded off to sleep.

Thirty minutes into the drive, Tom rose from a deep sleep to see a man dressed in white standing in the road. Tom turned to warn Kyle and shrieked when he saw that Kyle was fast asleep. Awakened by Tom's shriek, Kyle jerked the steering wheel, narrowly missing the man in the road. As the car flew past, the ghostly figure reached out and deftly opened Tom's door, pulling him from the car to a grassy embankment.

"Who are you?" Tom yelled.

"I am here to protect you," the figure said.

"Protection? You almost killed me," Tom shouted.

Then he heard squealing tires and the horn from a tractor-trailer, followed by the sickening impact of metal on metal.

"You were going down the wrong side of the interstate," said the figure, just before he disappeared.

Tom ran toward the crash. He found the steaming carnage, the burning rubber, and above all: death. He fell to his knees and began to vomit again.

Other cars stopped and tried to help, even though it was too late for his friends. Tom sat and cried as a passerby wrapped him in a blanket. Tom was shaken with fear at the way he had been spared.

Tom rubbed the bandage on his forehead as the funeral for his friends began. He had not been able to sleep since the accident. Withdrawal from the drugs wasn't helping. His father decided to take some time off from his heavy work schedule to be with his son. Lacy was away on an extended visit to her mother's house. Bryce's new priority showed him how bad the home situation had become.

Driving home, his father addressed the problem head on. "Son, you have a drug problem, and I'm willing to help you any way I can," he said, choking on his emotions.

"Screw you," Tom answered.

"I know I should have been around, but try not to hold that against me," Bryce said as tears trickled down his face. Tom stayed silent, staring out the window.

When they arrived home, they walked in together through the

garage. Tom stopped to admire his dad's prized possession, his new candy-apple red corvette. "She's a beauty," he said in a lighthearted tone.

"Yeah dad, she's beautiful," Tom replied, glancing at the car as he followed his dad into the house.

Tom laid in his bed and turned up his music. He sat up and began to think about his friends as the images in his head grew dark. "Death is your friend," Apollyon said as he dug his talons into Tom's skull. "It will stop this pain. You will finally sleep in peace."

Invisible to Tom, a male figure stood in the doorway. Rotting skin covered his pale face. He parted his raven black hair to reveal "SUICIDE" inscribed on his forehead.

"Is he ready for me?" Suicide asked Apollyon, .

"He's almost there. I have been working on him for years now," Apollyon said.

"It shouldn't take that long. Let me have him. He won't last a week," Suicide demanded.

"He's all yours. If you succeed, of course, it will be because of my efforts," Apollyon answered.

"Why do you say 'if'? Watch the power of my work," Suicide said, as a smile broke out over his face.

Unknown to the demons, another being listened from the other room with a very different plan. A smile spread across the angel's face.

Chapter 4
Tom's Drive

Tom approached the new Corvette convertible eagerly. The car's aluminum alloy wheels teased him. He slowly circled the car, adoring every detail. As he opened the door, he could smell the new leather seats. He eased into the driver's seat which folded around him with her comfortable fit. He gripped the wheel, feeling sheer delight at the way it felt an extension his hands.

He pushed in the clutch and turned the key. The motor roared awake; the beast was ready to rumble. He adjusted the rearview mirror and caught a glimpse of his own wavy dark hair. His smile spread across his face, reflecting the sheer excitement of this moment. He threw the car into gear, re-gripped the steering wheel, revved the engine and took off. The acceleration was mind numbing. *This is awesome*, he thought.

The car took to tight turns like it was on rails. Tom reveled in the snug seat as G-forces pulled on his body. "Whoa!" he shouted, part exclamation and part futile command. As he speed down the road, an onramp for the expressway beckoned to him and he could not resist it's allure. "Let's open up, baby, and see what you'll do," he said aloud. He punched the accelerator and watched his speed fly past 100 MPH. With little traffic and no police in sight, he was on the ride of his life.

In the distance, he saw a hitchhiker standing on the side of the road. The man caught his attention and they started a weird mutual stare down as Tom rapidly approached. The hitchhiker looked strangely familiar. He was tall, Caucasian-looking, and had wavy hair much like Tom's, but a bit more blonde. His eyes were a piercing blue; nothing escaped their gaze. As Tom forced his eyes away from the stranger, he noticed that the traffic in front of him had stopped. He slammed on his brakes, but not in time. Even with the Corvette's ABS, he knew he was going to hit the car stopped ahead. Suddenly and without thinking, he jerked the Corvette into the emergency lane, missing the car by inches. *How'd I do that?*

Tom waited for a few moments to catch his breath. *That was too close!* While the Corvette idled, recovering from its near-miss, the stranger strode up to the car, opened the door and slid in.

"Thanks for the ride," he said

"Who said I'm giving you a ride?" said Tom, shocked. *Who could believe the nerve of this stranger?*

"I'm just going up the street a little ways," the

stranger said, oblivious to Tom's reaction. Tom, dazed from the near-crash, sensed a greater danger if he didn't oblige.

"Ok," he said hesitantly.

"Great car," the stranger said. "I bet it's fast."

Gripping the wheel, Tom thought: *Maybe he's scared of speed. Let's see how long he lasts.* Tom blasted out of the emergency lane with everything the car had. With no effort, the car reached 100 mph again. The hitchhiker didn't seem to notice, much less care.

"My name is Trojol," the stranger said casually. Tom did not respond. "This is some car," Trojol said again. "You almost rammed that car back there,"

Tom remained silent, intent on driving at breakneck speed.

"Your brakes might not be working right," continued Trojol. "They get hot after a hard stop. It's called brake fade."

Great, now I have to listen to the world's expert on brakes. Just what I have always wanted, Tom thought. *Let's see what he thinks of this.* Tom slammed on his brakes. The pedal sank straight to the floor without slowing the car in the slightest. Now it was Tom who was scared. His pulse raced. He never had car trouble like this before; however, the stranger seemed not to notice.

"Beautiful day, isn't it?" Trojol interjected. Tom's mind was starting to panic. He grabbed the stick shift and tried to downshift. For some reason the car wouldn't shift gears. He grabbed the key to turn the car off, but it wouldn't budge.

Trojol continued talking, "The weather is so warm today." The terror rose in Tom when he noticed the car was speeding up. It had reached 120 mph and traffic was starting to thicken, causing him to dart in and out of lanes to avoid hitting the other cars. *This can't be happening!*

Trojol spoke up, "I know your brakes aren't working. In fact, there's something wrong with your car. Tom, this car is like your life. It's out of control. God wants to help direct your life but right now you are going the wrong direction."

Tom yelled back, "Well, why don't you do something to get me out of this crap."

Trojol spoke calmly, "It won't work with you driving. Let me have the wheel and I'll get you where you need to go."

Tom screamed, "Who are you?"

"I already told you, I am Trojol. God sent me to make sure you take the right path," said the angel.

"An angel?" Tom asked.

"Yes, I am an angel," he answered.

"I thought angels were supposed to say 'fear not' and all that crap," Tom asked.

"I am not a 'fear not' angel," Trojol replied

"Oh great. Everyone else gets a 'fear not' angel and I get a scare-the-crap-out-of-me angel," Tom stammered.

"I guess it is your lucky day," Trojol shot back.

"How come I don't feel so lucky?" Tom replied as he dodged another car.

The road was now full of cars. The corvette was traveling over 140 mph. Steering was becoming extremely difficult at this speed. As

Tom grasped the wheel, he glanced in his rear view mirror to see an ocean of blue and red lights following him. That's when he noticed the thumping sound of a helicopter which seemed to be hovering above them. Tom wanted to wipe his forehead but he didn't dare take his hands off the wheel. He was doing everything he could to keep the car on the road. Trojol seemed unconcerned about the fate of the vehicle. *Is this the death angel?* Tom thought to himself. *My life must be ending.*

"Trojol, how do I get right with God?" Tom asked, frantic now.

"Let me have the wheel," Trojol reiterated.

"Now?" Tom shouted. "Are you nuts?"

"Let go."

"Fine, we'll die together." Tom closed his eyes, released the wheel, and waited for the end.

Trojol grabbed the steering wheel and sharply spun it to the right. The Corvette spun wildly on the highway but never flipped. Screeching tires and smoke filled the air. The Corvette came to rest before an ocean of flashing lights. Tom couldn't believe he was still alive. Stranger still, Trojol was now in the driver's seat, and Tom was in the passenger seat.

Gunning the engine, Trojol aimed the Corvette straight for the police phalanx. But at the moment of impact, the line of law enforcement parted like the Red Sea before Moses, and the Corvette was once more on the open road. In a beautiful display of highway choreography, Trojol had the 'Vette purring at 160 mph as every obstacle faded from sight. Tom took his first deep breath since Trojol had entered the car. Yet the adventure was not over by a long shot. Another round of shock and awe awaited him just around the bend.

A large body of water appeared on both sides of the highway. As he stared a moment longer, Tom saw a bridge in the distance—a drawbridge rising from the middle as a ship passed underneath.

"Aren't you going to slow down?," Tom asked. Trojol calmly shifted gears and the Corvette leapt forward.

Near the mouth of the rapidly approaching bridge, Tom saw three hearses parked in the road. *Oh great, now we're playing "chicken."* As the

'Vette accelerated, Tom closed his eyes and faced his fears. He saw the brevity of his life and the many mistakes he had made. For the second time that day, he thought: *"Am I going to die?"*

As if he read Tom's mind, Trojol answered calmly, "Yes, you are."

Trojol corrected his approach to strike the middle hearse, leaving no chance for a sudden turn or stop. The hearses stood firm as the Corvette slammed into the black metal. Tom felt the impact, but there was no pain, only twisting metal and shattering glass just like his other accidents. The Corvette's frame slowly bent and the windshield started its cracking pattern piece by piece. Tom felt himself gradually falling into the exploding air bag.

A second later, Tom opened his eyes to see the hearses in the side-view mirror. The one in the middle looked to be flattened by a tank. "How did that...," he started to ask, but something in angel's face stopped him.

"Death is upon you," Trojol said, turning his gaze upon Tom. Tom looked down at his clothes. They had turned a ghostly white. "I thought you were going to save me," he shouted. Then he saw the bridge looming before them.

It had fully risen now to allow the ship to pass. "You're not going to jump that, are you?" Tom yelled, already guessing the answer.

"What do you care? You're dead," answered Trojol.

The 'Vette was now traveling over 200 mph. Tom didn't think the car could go that fast, but nothing about this trip made any sense. In a split-second decision, his elected to keep his eyes wide open, and regretted it immediately. The car went airborne and seemed to float for an eternity. Adding to the excitement, the car started flipping and turning.

Trojol raised his arms and shouted, "I love this car." Fortunately, the seat belt held Tom from falling out, aided by his iron clad grip on whatever parts remained intact.

Beer bottles, drugs in baggies, bloody cotton balls and other icons of Tom's rebellious life were gently falling from the car as it continued it's slippery spiral. Tom stared in sickened amazement as the items fell into the bay. Then, without warning, the car landed upright on hard road, jarring Tom's teeth and throwing his frame of reference past comprehension.

People clothed all in white stood on both sides of the road and applauded his landing. Their faces looked normal—from every walk of life—yet none were recognizable.

"Who are they?" Tom asked, half to himself.

"These are your new friends," Trojol said.

Amazingly, the car was still traveling. Any normal car would have been destroyed, but this one did not display a scratch. The highway was now almost empty. Trojol exclaimed, "Here's our exit," And jerked the wheel.

From where Tom sat, there was no exit, only dense forest. Yet that didn't stop this angel. He plowed straight through it, weaving between trees, knowing exactly when and where to turn. It was as if he had driven this route many times before.

Out of nowhere, a small country church appeared. It had white siding with a few windows and fit well in the rural setting. The steeple was crowned with a simple cross. The gravel surrounding the building suggested, "Park anywhere." And the two dozen cars outside had done just that. From the faint sound of music, Tom could tell a meeting was still in progress. Trojol slammed on the brakes, and the car slid to a halt. As Tom stared at the church, Trojol vanished without a word, and the ride was over.

Tom saw people running from the church, coming to see if he was all right. One of them said, "Son, you look pale." Tom tried to get out of the car. The whole ordeal had left him dizzy, disoriented, and nauseous.

Attempting to walk, Tom lost his balance and fell. He closed his eyes for a brief moment.

Tom was now laying on the floor of a drug rehabilitation center. He sat up and realized the whole car scene was a dream. He had never taken that drive in his dad's corvette. It was all in his mind, yet it was so vivid. He broke down in tears. He felt cold and weak as he shook.

The dream was true: his life indeed was out of control. Questions raced through his mind. *Was this dream warning of his death or was it a promise of a new life? What was the hidden message? Who is Trojol?*

Tom ignored the sweat and vomit covering his shirt. His thoughts had no room for anything but the dream.

He got up off the floor and dragged himself to the sink. He washed his face and looked in the mirror. He saw his roughly shaven face, matted down hair, and bags under his eyes. As he contemplated how awful he looked, he saw the reflection of a man standing by his bed. He turned in a panic, but no one there was there. Tom started to shake again.

I must be going crazy. I swear there was someone there.

He rang for the nurse's call button. "Nurse, there was someone in my room. Can you come here?" Tom shouted in a frenzy.

"Coming," said the bored voice on the other end.

At the nurse's station, the nurses started joking. "We got a live one in room 138. He'll probably be calling you all night. Welcome to the Psych ward, Tracy."

Maybe he just needs something to calm his nerves, she thought.

The nurses reminded her, "Make sure someone is with you when you go into the room." Tracy radioed for the doctor and an orderly. They peaked into Tom's room through the heavy glass window. He was pacing the floor frantically.

"I've never seen heroin withdrawal like this," Tracy said.

"I've seen it worse," answered the doctor. "Get a dose of methadone. He needs rest."

"Right away," Said Tracy.

With the medicine at the ready, the group entered Tom's room together.

"It's about time. What took you so long?" demanded Tom.

The doctor spoke in a soothing voice said, "Tom, please sit down. I have your medicine."

"What are you going to do about the man in my room?"

"What man are you talking about, Tom?" asked Tracy.

"There was a man in the bathroom mirror. He was standing by my bed," Tom jetted.

The doctor continued in his calm tone, "Tom, there is no one else in the room. Besides, you don't have a bathroom mirror. We took them out last year," the doctor said.

"There's a mirror in this bathroom, right here," Tom said as he tried to open the locked door. "He's probably hiding in there."

The nurse looked at the doctor, who nodded. She pulled out a key and unlocked the door. It was just a storage closet. There was no mirror. It wasn't even a bathroom.

"I'm not crazy, I'm not! I know what I saw," cried Tom.

"You're not crazy, Tom. Heroin withdrawal makes you think you see strange things. They're hallucinations," the doctor said, trying to diffuse the situation. "Tom, please sit down. I have your methadone shot. This will help you finish your sleep tonight. It'll help you relax," the doctor said, nodding at the nurse once more.

Tom realized that he wasn't getting anywhere with them. "Ok, I'll sit down, shut up, and take my medicine like a good boy, but I'm telling you someone was here in this room," Tom said dejectedly.

"Oh, we believe you Tom. Sit still and give me your arm," Tracy the nurse said as she administered the shot.

As Tom reclined, he started feeling the effects of the methadone quickly. *Maybe I did imagine it,* his calmer mind said. Then he glanced at the night stand and saw a set of car keys with a Corvette logo. He jerked upright and started to scream, but the methadone pulled him back down. In his becalmed state, he could hear the orderlies talking just outside his door.

"Somebody tore the crap out of that Corvette. It looked like they drove the freaking thing through the forest. How stupid is that?" one of them said.

Tom wept as he realized that no one believed him. Then he thought of God. Tom prayed with renewed desperation as a large angel in the storage closet smiled broadly.

Chapter 5
Tom's Bridge to Recovery

After he woke up, Tom asked to speak with a pastor. The staff asked who he wanted but Tom didn't know. The staff remembered there was a volunteer who also pastored a small church outside of town.

Bill Hampton was called that day and came over immediately. Bill was a large man with a swarthy and wrinkled skin. His grip was firm even though his crew cut had turned gray. He had been a hard working farmer most of his adult life. Bill was a 'down home' guy; a loyal friend with a soft heart.

Bill turned to ministry after a tragic event in his family. It helped him find answers for himself and others. After some small talk, Tom started to open up to him. "I am so messed up. I have so much anger. I feel hatred for everyone. I've been faking it for so long that I don't know who I really am. Can you help me?"

As he listened, Bill's eyes filled with tears. Tom gradually stopped talking and waited for Bill's response. Bill asked, "Do you think that God loves you?" Tom didn't know what to think. He had not thought about God's love as being important to him.

"I don't know," Tom answered.

"Well, you probably know that Jesus Christ died for you so that you could be forgiven and given a new life in Him. He can heal all the scars of your past and fix the mess you have found yourself in. But you have to give your heart to Him and trust Him to do all this for you."

"Is it really that simple?" Tom asked.

"That's where it starts, Tom," Bill said. They prayed together, and for the first time in Tom's life, he gave something to God—himself.

Something new came into Tom's life–a peace he couldn't explain. It was too much to understand, yet he enjoyed it. Bill talked with him for another hour. There was a connection between the two men that continued throughout the weeks of Tom's treatment.

After 12 weeks, the psychologists released Tom. His dad and Bill were there to greet him. Tom told Bill that he would like to go to his church but that he didn't have a car anymore. Bill offered to loan him one. He also offered Tom a part-time job at the church and a place to stay until he could get on his feet again.

Tom gladly accepted both. His dad knew enough not to interfere in his recovery and reluctantly agreed that he needed to be on his own. Tom caught a ride with Bill to the church. As they drove through the hilly mountain roads, things started to look very familiar. "It's like I've seen this before," Tom said.

"Well, we're almost at the church," said Bill.

As they turned the corner, Tom's face grew pale.

"Tom, are you OK?" Bill said.

Tom's eyes scanned every detail of the church building.

"Tom, what's the matter?"

"I have been here before. I saw this church weeks ago in a dream that really messed me up. I can't believe this is happening," Tom said through his cracking voice.

"That's awesome, Tom. I've never heard of anything like that before. God is arranging things in your life!"

Tom sat for awhile and just let everything sink in. This was indeed the start of a new life.

Bill showed Tom the church and the parsonage out back. Many of the things he saw were like flashbacks to his dream. *How did I have a dream that showed this place?* He thought.

Bill showed him the office.

"What are these?" Tom asked.

"They are the baptism robes. Tom do you know what baptism is?"

"I'm not sure. I never paid much attention in church to those kinds of things."

"It's what God commanded us to do after we believe in Christ. It is our public profession of faith," Bill said.

"I have seen these robes before. In the dream, I had one of these on and I asked the angel if I was dead and he said yes. What does that mean? Am I going to die soon?"

"Baptism is symbolic just like dreams are symbolic. We have died with Christ and are raised with Him in Baptism. We received His Life for our resurrection. Your dream was teaching you this and foretelling that baptism was going to be in your future. What else did your dream say?"

"I don't know. I don't even remember it all. It comes in pieces when I see reminders, like this robe," Tom said.

"Tom, would you like to get baptized tomorrow during church service? The congregation would love to meet you,"

"Who am I to resist my future?" answered Tom with a grin.

The next day, Tom came to the church service. And once again, surprises came. He sat on the last row, ashamed to be there. His life was so different from these people. He had hated church and despised Christians. Now, he was one of them and it felt awkward.

Everyone welcomed him in as if he was family. They shook his hand, hugged him, and even prayed for him. Some cried for joy that he was finally there. As they talked with him, Tom's eyes grew large when he realized that he had seen these people before. They were ones dressed in white robes on the side of the road cheering when his car jumped the bridge.

As he sat down, still in shock, a man approached him. "Son, are you Ok? You look really pale."

Tom started crying. He realized God had brought him these people because he was going to need a lot of love and reassurance. God loved him that much. This was the missing piece in his life. *Could God be this good to me?* He knew the answer.

The service began as the people started singing songs of praise. Tom praised God from his heart for the first time. He felt a strange presence—the same peace as when we accepted Christ. He noticed a mystical look on the people's faces as they sang. It was as if they were seeing heaven.

After a few songs, Bill stepped forward to give his sermon. "God has a weakness for you. He longs to be close to you. He loves you and is speaking to your heart. He will never leave you or forsake you. His kindness is forever to those who turn to Him."

Tom had never heard preaching about God being so personal, so loving and kind. This was a crash-course on the goodness of God. Then he thought of the Corvette dream and laughed out loud. Crash-course…good one, God.

The time of baptism came and Bill invited Tom forward. "Tom, would you like to tell the folks a little about your journey to this decision?" Bill asked.

"Uh, yeah I guess so. I don't really know where to start," Tom said sheepishly. "My life was out of control. I never really liked church. When I started using heavily, I knew I needed to slow down but I couldn't. I checked myself into rehab. Then I had a dream that this angel was trying to talk some sense into me. I realize now that God gave me that dream to show me that He already had my life planned out. I met Bill shortly after that and I gave my life to Christ."

Bill spoke up, "Tom, we are going to be a family to you. We are going to help you get back up on your feet. We have been praying for someone just like you."

As Tom looked into the congregation, several heads nodded in agreement, and he saw a few eyes misting with emotion.

"Tom, I baptize you in the name of the Father, and of the Son, and of the Holy Spirit," Bill recited as he dunked Tom into the water. When Tom came out, Bill said, "Tom, your past is behind you. It is all washed away. You are one of God's children now. He will begin to make himself more real to you every day." Tom and Bill embraced. Tom was home.

In the coming months, Tom did his best to adjust to his new life. He learned many things from Bill. He learned how to swim and fish. He also learned that you can't do both at the same time. He planted a garden and grew tomatoes, peas, green beans, and potatoes. The simple life was refreshing for him as he battled the addictions. Worse than the physical addictions were the attitudes that still poisoned his mind and heart. Although Christ had changed so much in his life, the Lord was pruning many more areas. One area was his anger. Tom had to learn contentment. As he did, the Lord's presence met with him.

He also learned the Bible. Bill was a fanatic about it. Every day there were Bible drills. Tom had to memorize scripture after scripture. These verses brought out questions in Tom. "Bill, why did God do all those things for me and not for others?"

Many times, Bill did not know how to answer, but they studied to find the answers together. As time went on, Bill and Tom became deeper friends.

"Tom, you are so much like my son. I wish you could have met him. He died five years ago," Bill confided.

"What happened?" Tom asked.

"He was into drugs. I prayed for him every night for many years and it seemed like nothing happened. One day, he was gunned down by a dealer. I can't help blaming myself for how things turned out in his life. Having you here is like having my son back. I thank God for you," Bill said tearfully.

"I wish I could do better than I do. I am really struggling with this whole thing. I wish I could have done something for your son," Tom said.

"There's something else." Bill said softly. "I have cancer. I am dying. I was given a few years to live. I haven't told my congregation yet. They know that I have had some health problems. I guess what bothers me the most is not knowing whether I will see my son in heaven. I suppose I won't. He fought the call of God his whole life. I couldn't persuade him to serve Christ. I feel like such a failure," Bill said.

"Dude, you are the coolest person I know. You have nothing to be ashamed of. You've helped so many people. Everybody loves you. You're an awesome man. Is there anything we can do to fight this cancer?" Tom asked.

"I just want someone with me when I die," Bill answered.

"I'll be with you," Tom said. "But hey, don't die on me today, OK? Let's go do something fun. What do you say?"

Bill tossed Tom the keys to the car. "I'm too tired. But why don't you go see high bridge? It's the tallest railroad bridge over a navigable river. There is a nice park. You can just relax, pray, and have a peaceful lunch."

"Sounds great," Tom replied.

Tom packed a lunch, grabbed a Bible, and jumped in the car. Bill waved goodbye, but was hit with a weird feeling of impending doom as Tom drove off. "What is it, God?" Bill asked quietly, but there was no reply. Just the feeling, and it was growing stronger. Bill started praying. Since the last thing he remembered was saying goodbye to Tom, he concluded that Tom was going to be in some type of danger. The feeling continued to dog him as he prayed for Tom's protection. He started to weep. The experience was being guided. There seemed to be no explanation, only the stern feeling that he was to continue praying.

As Tom drove, he enjoyed the beautiful day. The sunshine and breeze were intoxicating. The flowering hardwoods were in full bloom on the rolling hills. Tom didn't think much of Bill's old Buick LeSabre, but at least an angel wasn't at the wheel.

As Tom continued down the road, he started daydreaming. As he rounded a curve, a car from behind tried to pass him, driving erratically.

The car clipped Tom's front bumper as it passed, cutting Tom off. Enraged, Tom hit the gas and started to chase the offending car.

Road rage took over and dictated the plans from there. The two cars sped dangerously down the winding roads. Despite their twisting and turning, there was someone riding on top of Tom's car.

Broadly displayed for no one to see, the guardian was enjoying his ride on top. What both road ragers did not know was that there was a sharp turn into the park. They both skidded off the road as the high bridge stood in the background. The other driver took off running, and he carried a young boy. Tom ran after him. The man was running toward the bridge.

"You'll pay for this, jerk," Tom shouted.

"Back off! Or the kid gets thrown off the bridge," the man threatened. Instead of scaring Tom, the threat just made him angrier.

"The hell you will," Tom shouted back.

The man climbed onto the bridge with the frantically struggling boy. Tom chased them onto the bridge. As they ran, a dozen police cars pulled into the park with their sirens blazing.

"There he is. Who is chasing him? Get him. And protect the hostage," the police captain shouted over the radio. *What is he doing?* The captain whispered. Over the bullhorn, the police shouted for the men to freeze. Neither obeyed.

Near the middle of the bridge, as Tom gained on the man, he suddenly stopped, causing Tom to crash into him. The boy broke free but was too scared to run down the tracks.

Tom and the stranger began trading blows while struggling to keep their balance on the narrow train tracks. As Tom glanced down at the water, the man hit Tom hard, knocking him down. Instantly Tom knew him. It was Gill.

Gill tried to roll Tom off the bridge, but Tom grabbed his leg and tripped him. Now they both rolled to where they were hanging on the edge of the bridge, continuing to kick each other.

The tracks started to vibrate. The two men looked up to see the train approaching in the distance. Tom tried to pull himself up to help the boy, but Gill managed to pull himself up first. He smiled at Tom and said, "I should have killed you when I had the chance." Gill struck Tom hard, knocking him down again. As Tom hung from the bridge, Gill tried to stomp his hands. Tom kept changing grip, remembering the dream from long ago. Tom held on for a few more seconds until his strength gave out. "God, I'm sorry. Forgive me. Save me. I'm yours." Tom's grip slowly loosened and his plunge began.

The train was almost on top of Gill and the boy, when two guardians appeared. One stood close to the frightened boy.

"Hey, little fella, ever ridden on a train before?" the guardian asked as he grabbed the boy's hand. The boy shook his head no, and gazed into the face of the angel.

An instant later, the guardian hoisted the boy into his arms and onto the front grill of the oncoming train, unscathed.

The second guardian made a nose dive from the bridge and plunged faster than gravity could allow. He caught Tom in his arms in midair and the two plunged into the shallow water. The impact of the water rendered Tom unconscious.

Gill fell from the bridge and plunged into the water below, dying instantly.

The boy's anxious parents stood with the police, watching the drama unfold from the park. As the train crossed the river, the boy jumped off the slowing train, rolled into the weeds, and stood up unhurt. He ran to meet parents as they rushed toward him with open arms, crying tears of joy. The stunned police officers could only stammer.

"Did that just happen?" the captain asked the sergeant.

"I think so," the sergeant muttered.

Shaking off his disbelief, the captain ordered a search party to the river to retrieve the two bodies. Within hours, both of the fallen were found. Gill's body was pulled from the water. Tom—to everyone's amazement—was found lying on the river bank unconscious. As the emergency crew revived him, he was to disorientated to tell them what happened. He could barely remember his name. Fortunately, Bill's phone number in Tom's wallet had not washed out. He handed it to the police and they called Bill.

"We have a Tom Johnson. He says he knows you. He was in an accident. He seems to be OK, but we are sending him to Metro hospital to get checked out. He's stable, just really shaken up."

"Thank you officer, I'll be right there. Thank God that's he's alive," Bill said.

When Tom woke up in the hospital, Bill was with him.

"Where am I? Who are you?" Tom asked.

"Tom, it's me Bill. You remember me, don't you? You were in some kind of accident. The police said that you fell from the bridge. Tom, do you know how I am?"

"Bill, Bill, yes! Bill I remember. I'm sorry I wrecked your car. I don't know what got into me. I'm so stupid." Tom cried.

"That car was a piece of junk. I just kept it because it was my son's. I'll get another one. No big deal. You're OK, that's all that matters. The police said you fell over 900 feet? That's humanly impossible. There must have been angels around you or something. There is no way you should have survived that fall. The other guy died instantly."

"I don't really remember what happened. I'll take your word for it. I guess I was just lucky." Tom said.

"Luck had nothing to do with this. God saved your life. There must be a huge calling on your life. These kinds of things didn't happen around me until you showed up," Bill said.

"I don't know what to say. I've done so many bad things. Why would God choose me?"

"I don't know. But there is no denying it," Bill said confidently.

"Well, who am I to argue with you about it?"

Chapter 6
Ann Wentworth

Ann Wentworth perused the library of her New York City townhome, trying to find her college textbook on mergers and acquisitions. She hadn't been in her library in a year, ever since becoming CEO for Star Oil. Now she struggled to find time for anything but work. She pulled open her Harvard Yearbook and found her picture. She looked through the signatures and recalled fondly the names and faces, basking in the memory of that idealistic time. She earned an MBA with a 4.0 grade point average and was ready to set the world aflame.

Between the pages, Ann found the offer letter from Boston Consulting Group—her first job after college. Oh, the excitement of that first big step into a successful career. She fumbled through more books, finding the ones she had purchased to learn the Oil and Gas industry, and a piece of paper fell out from one.

It was an old love letter from her husband John, who had been an oil rig supervisor. She laughed at the goofy poem he wrote, enjoying his gruff but endearing approach to life. She relaxed as she reminisced about their wedding and the early years of marriage.

John's peaceful soul always seemed to calm her, and these days, she needed to be calmed often. In the midst of her reverie, she looked up and saw the book she had been searching for. It had been so close yet she couldn't see it. She grabbed it and muttered, "It's about time."

Trojol sat unseen beside her, gazing lovingly at the woman he had been assigned to guard. Ann didn't see him but felt something very different. She shook her head and left the room. The angel smiled and said, "Sweet dreams."

As Ann slipped into bed, she turned to the breathing mound of covers next to her. "Honey, does this room feel creepy to you?"

"What do you mean?" John replied groggily.

"It just feels weird. I can't explain it."

"Get some rest. You've got a long day tomorrow."

"I'm not crazy," she retorted.

"I'm not saying you're crazy. I'm just saying get some sleep. OK?"

"Ok," she snapped back.

Ann laid down and fell asleep quickly. Later that night, she heard a sound coming from the back door. John was deep in his snores, so she rose up to see what was going on. As she walked in the kitchen, she saw that the back door was open. For some reason, she felt no fear.

Now she could hear voices through the door. Her curiosity got the best of her and she through the door and discovered the entrance to a cave. *Where did this come from?* She thought. The voices she was hearing came from inside the cave. She slowly crept into the darkened cave. She squinted her eyes as they adjusted to the dim light. She rubbed the damp walls as water droplets fell into her curly blonde hair. She moved her bare feet slowly across the sandy soil. She thought the voices were getting closer. She was startled when a woman standing next to her spoke.

"Ann, I'm Susan Fillmore. Watching your daughter grow has been such fun. I helped her learn to walk."

"Ma'am, I don't know who you are but I don't have a daughter. In fact, I can't have children," Ann relied.

Susan just smiled and disappeared. Ann rubbed her eyes in disbelief. She turned and gasped to see another person standing behind her.

"I'm sorry I startled you, Ann. I'm Rita Small. I'm a friend of your grandmother. Ann, you are so pretty. Your daughter looks so much like you," said the lady.

"I don't have a daughter! Don't you people get it?" Ann shot back.

"Her hair is just like yours, and you have the same chin. It's remarkable," Rita said, ignoring Ann's assertion.

The woman disappeared. Ann started to shake as she searched for a way out. She started back but found that the cave seemed different. Instead of the entrance, she ran into another woman.

"Ann, is that you? Remember me. I'm Sandy White. I was your teacher in high school. You were so smart, just like your daughter. She has such a curiosity to know everything. You really should see her. She's close. I just saw her a minute ago," the strange woman replied.

"I don't have a daughter. You people are crazy!" she shrieked.

Ann's thoughts were becoming scattered. She was becoming irrational and knew it. She needed to get out fast, but how? Ann started running but felt instantly fatiqued. She pushed her legs harder but got nowhere. She finally saw a light ahead. Time seemed to stop as her legs wilted like overcooked spaghetti. Her resolve was falling like the stock price of a bankrupt company.

As strange as things were, Ann was not prepared for what happened next. As Ann pushed her shaky legs, she came face to face with a girl about 18 years old. Ann gasped in horror. The resemblance was unmistakable. Ann froze, unable to move or talk.

"Mom, is that you?" the girl asked. Ann was speechless. "Mom, I want you to know that I love you. I am in heaven. I love you so much and miss you dearly," the girl said as she faded away.

Ann stared into the darkness; horror gripped her. Ann could do nothing but breathe as her heart pounded and her mind shutdown on overload. She was completely overwhelmed—a rare occurrence for the CEO of a multi-national oil company. But she was not in charge here.

Ann fell to the damp, cold ground and cried. While she closed her eyes, the floor seemed to change under her, becoming warmer and softer. She heard a familiar voice, one she trusted and loved.

"Honey, are you ok?"

It was John. Ann sat up in bed and continued crying. He reached out to embrace her. "It's a just a bad dream, dear. You're ok."

She struggled to speak through her tears. "John, it was so horrible. I was stuck in this cave. It was so real. I saw a girl." She stopped talking, interrupted by a fresh spasm of anguish. "It was so horrible. I can't talk about it," she said.

"You're ok now. I'll stay up with you if you want," John reassured her.

"I'd like that," she said, forcibly trying to calm down. He held her for a long time, then he thought of something that would take her mind off the dream.

"I'll get you something to eat," he said, springing from the bed.

"OK. Thanks. Anything but spaghetti, OK?"

John always seemed to know how to help her. Not many people knew or saw her weak side.

John walked to the kitchen, breezing right past Trojol. John sensed something but quickly dismissed it. Trojol smiled and left the house.

He would return many times, bringing more dreams that would continue to shake Ann to her core. Ann's healing had begun, but it didn't feel like that to her, at least not yet. It was to be an excruciating process, but God's love conquers all, and He would leave no stone unturned in His glorious quest to save Ann's whole heart.

The next day, Ann tried to forget the dream, but she couldn't shake it. On the way to work, she noticed her hands shaking. *I'm not letting that cursed dream get to me. Just forget it, Ann. It's just a dream. It's just random neurons firing in my brain.* Yet the dream sequence last night was anything but random. Ann knew it, but that didn't stop her from fighting it. With considerable effort, she was able to concentrate on her work, and gradually the turmoil subsided.

She was preparing an offer to purchase her company's main rival, West Texas Oil Company. In an effort to convince her board, she had prepared over 200 pages of legal documents for a presentation today, meticulously laying out options from stock swaps to bank loans.

As she forced herself to maintain an ironclad grip on her "perfect" world, she did not realize how trapped in a cage of pain and isolation she was. God alone held the keys of freedom, and what God had planned for her was so much better.

She arrived at the corporate headquarters in Manhattan, anxious to deliver the information to the board. She paused a second and closed her eyes to gather herself. But when she did, the images of the cave would rush back into her mind. She could still hear the voices calling to her.

I'm not going crazy. I'm not going crazy. Why am I obsessing over this stupid dream?

She didn't know there was someone right beside her, feeding her thoughts. It was God's messenger, Trojol. Since Ann had no understanding of the spiritual realm, she was defenseless against the angel of God's love.

The day dragged on. The board launched an endless barrage of questions, challenges, feints and dodges. Ann knew it was going to be easy, but she grew impatient, so she suggested a twenty minute break. The board members continued reading the proposal and looked at the options while Ann excused herself. As she walked down the hall, people started looking like the people in the dream. Her heart skipped when a woman passed by who had hair similar to her "daughter". The face was different, but it still disturbed her.

She couldn't escape. Her world was caving in around her. Distraught, she headed back to the board room—to the "devil she knew"—to endure three more hours of battle. At the end of the day, her mind was shot and her energy was drained.

As Ann drove home, nothing seemed to refresh her. She turned the radio on. Even her favorite music didn't seem to help. Trojol smiled as he sat in her car undetected. He knew she was going to be a tough nut to crack. The Lord had already told him so. He was confident in the Holy Spirit's efforts, and he continued his assignment with great care and joy.

Entering the safety of her house, she broke down and cried. Her husband held her and asked, "What, again? Ann, what is going on?"

"It was awful," she said.

"What happened? Were you fired? Did they turn down your proposal?" he asked.

"No, nothing like that. It's that cursed dream. I can't get it out of my head," she sputtered.

"Hey, why don't you take tomorrow off? We'll get a bite to eat at the Tavern on the Green. What do you think?" he offered.

"I would like that," she said, calming down.

"Well, then it's a date," he said.

The next day was better for Ann. The dream was not frightening. She noticed that when she tried to forget the dream, her emotions got worse, but when she allowed herself to contemplate it, she felt a strange peace drawing her to a unseen destination.

Amidst this calm, Ann determined to remember the dream's details and face the many questions that intrigued her. As she and John ate lunch, she floated an idea. "I was thinking that maybe I should talk to a psychologist about my dream. Maybe an expert on dreams."

"I think that's a great idea. Are you going to finish your lobster?" he asked.

"Get your own lobster," she snapped with a smile.

"Scott may know someone," he said.

At last, Ann started to feel good again. She relaxed and took a long breath. As she pursued the dream, she felt she was being somehow rewarded. She had no idea how deep the dream was or how much she needed to explore to find its meaning. Standing by, Trojol just smiled. This was what he enjoyed about being a messenger of God.

With encouragement from her husband and the strong recommendation of a friend, and despite her initial willingness, Ann reluctantly agreed to see a psychologist. Greg Fillmore had a Doctorate in Psychology with an emphasis in dream theory. He was recognized by his peers as a leader in the field. Greg was ready for anyone and any dream. That was, until he met Ann.

As Ann approached the desk, the secretary pointed her and John to the waiting room. "Doctor Fillmore be with you in a few minutes; please have a seat."

Instead, Ann paced the floor.

"I don't have much time. Is there some way to hurry things along?" She said to the officious secretary.

"He will be with you soon. I'll let him know you're here," the secretary said.

Ann reluctantly sat down, stared ahead for a moment, then unsheathed her smart phone. She checked her voice mail messages, then began sending emails.

John said, "Ann, I know you're anxious about this, but he may be able to help you."

"We'll see about that. First of all, I am not crazy. Secondly, this guy is probably some kind of quack that will hypnotize me into buying something."

"Please Ann, just relax. This is not going to hurt," John said, trying to calm her.

"That's what the doctor says right before he injects the 12 inch needle into your leg," she said. The remark caught him as funny and he started laughing, which made her smile a little, despite her best intentions.

"Ok, just try it. If it doesn't help, we'll do something else," John said.

Before she could shoot back another response, the secretary announced: "Doctor Fillmore will see you now. Please come with me." Ann marched to the psychologist room.

She burst through the door and exclaimed, "I'm here and I hope this won't take long."

"Ann Wentworth, I'm Doctor Greg Fillmore. You can call me Greg. Please sit down and relax. I've got a few questions for you."

Greg asked many questions about Ann's background and personality. It didn't take him long to realize the person that Ann was.

"Why don't you tell me why you are here," Greg inquired.

That question broke the ice into small pieces. Ann was being asked to reveal her vulnerability.

"About 3 weeks ago, I had a dream, but it was more than just a dream. It was so vivid and frightening. I kept seeing segments of it in other dreams. Sometimes I have the same dream again. It's confusing, distracting, and interfering with my work. It won't leave my head."

Greg listened carefully and contemplated her statements in the quiet space between them. Finally, he spoke.

"Well, Ann. May I call you Ann?" he asked.

"Yes, that's fine," she said.

"Ann, this is very normal. I know many people who have repetitive dreams. Of course, each one is different. But by observing the dream, I can help you make sense of it and find some peace. Dreams of this kind are often messages about something that you're not facing in your waking life. There are different theories about why we have them. My personal belief is that some dreams are messages from God. He is personally speaking to you about something that may be a life or death situation. Do you have a religious background?" he asked.

"No," Ann answered.

"That's OK. As long as you can entertain the idea that this dream may be coming from God, then it will be fine for our discussion. Can I count on this? He asked.

"Why not," Ann said, surprising herself.

After Ann described the dream in detail, Greg had an idea.

"Ann, since our time for today is drawing to a close, I have an assignment for you. First—these people you saw—try to remember them. Write down everything about them. Their names, where they lived, the clothes they wore, what they said, who or what they represent to you. Second—see if there is some kind of link between them. It will probably take you a little while to do this. Let's meet again in two weeks. If the dreams start getting worse or if you need to see me for another reason, call me.

Also, if the dreams go away for awhile, it doesn't mean that they are gone. You have to resolve the underlying issues to make them stop. Again, I want you to know that what is happening to you is not a bad thing. It is a message God is using to help you," Greg added.

Ann felt at peace, relieved that she was not going crazy and that this may be a message from God. Greg's approach seemed to make sense. "Ok, I'll see you in two weeks," she said.

As she left Greg's office, John noticed that her demeanor had changed. He thought he actually saw a smirk on her determined mouth.

"Do I see a smile, Mrs. Ann Wentworth?" he asked.

Her smile broadened as she said, "Shut up. Are you taking me out tonight or what?"

"I thought you'd never ask," he said, smiling back.

At the restaurant, she explained to him about the session. Despite the urge to label the psychologist's request for research as quackery, Ann started her quest to learn more about the people and symbols in her dream. The first person was Susan Fillmore. She had been dressed in a old fashioned dress that Ann remembered from her days as a college student.

She found out Susan's biography—where she lived, when she was born, when she died, etc. Nothing about the information seemed out of place. She was born in 1930. She died in 1982. She made a career as a daycare operator, and she loved infants. She was an avid church member and she ran the infant ministry. In the dream, Susan told Ann that her daughter had just learned how to walk. That was something that a toddler would do. Although this information was forming patterns, the meaning of the dream was still hidden. Within a week, however, things would start to change.

The second person in the cave was Rita Small. Again, she was a childcare worker who loved infants and toddlers. She was younger than Rita. She was born in 1954 and died of cancer in 1983. She was also a volunteer at church, caring for infants and toddlers. Her words in the dream were about Ann's daughter's physical looks. With each person, a pattern emerged. They all died early. They died sequentially. They spoke of things that would normally happen in each stage of a child's development.

Instead of answering questions for Ann, these pieces of information puzzled her more, filling her with an endless stream of questions. When she met again with the psychologist two weeks later, he was encouraged by Ann's diligence and the thoroughness of her research. As the two of them reviewed the information, he was astonished at the dream's intricate and consistent details.

"This dream is beyond anything I have ever seen before. This is definitely from God. He is trying to tell you something," Greg exclaimed.

As Ann sat and thought, her face turned pale. "All of these people died early. Am I going to die or something? Is God going to kill me for something? I don't think I have done anything deserving of that," she said, starting to panic.

"Dreams like this are definitely warnings of some kind. It may or may not be warning you of impending tragedy. But there is something important that you need to make a decision on. It is very important to God and you." Greg concluded.

These words struck fear in Ann and she fought back, as was her typical response. "You are so full of crap. I'm sorry I came here. Goodbye," She said as she bolted for the door.

"Ann, please don't leave," Greg said, but it was too late. She was already out the door.

John was waiting for her. "That was quick. Are you ok?" he asked.

"We are finished here. I'll talk about it in the car," she fumed as she stormed towards the door.

"Mrs. Wentworth, do you want to schedule a follow-up

appointment?" the secretary asked as Ann shot by. Ann ran to the car, cursing all the way. Her husband knew his wife didn't normally act like this. Something spooked her.

"Honey, do you want to go out somewhere tonight?" he asked trying to settle her down.

"How can you think of food at a time like this?" she said.

"What happened in there?" he demanded.

"That quack of yours said that 'God' is warning me but couldn't tell me what is was. He'll probably say he can figure it out for say fifty-thousand dollars. I knew this whole thing was a rip-off," she retorted.

"He said that about God?" he asked. "How did he get God out of a cave dream?" John asked.

"I don't know. He just did," she said.

John reached out and held his wife.

"Hey, last I checked, God is a good God. I'm sure that if this is from Him, then He is only trying to help. Do you want to talk to a minister or something?"

Although Ann was starting to calm down, anything to do with God was not a good idea for her right now.

"I want to eat at the Waldorf tonight," she said abruptly.

"Now that's my girl," was his heartfelt reply.

Although the two were in the car together, they were not alone. Trojol was seated in the back. He had already made reservations for someone else to meet them at dinner.

As they were seated at their table, Ann told John what to order for her, and went to the lounge in the lobby. As she was seated, an older man approached her.

"Ann, is that you?" he asked. He looked somewhat familiar to her but she couldn't place him.

"Can I help you with something?" she politely replied.

"Ann, I don't know if you remember me. I'm Brian Wheeler. I was your high school principal. I helped you get into Harvard," he said proudly.

"Mr. Wheeler, Is that really you? You look great. What are you up to these days?"

"I quit teaching and went into ministry. I am at the hotel next door for a minister's conference and wandered in to see the legendary Waldorf."

"Well I'm glad you did," she replied.

As they talked, Ann felt the freedom to tell her old principal about the dream and what the psychologist said. Brian Wheeler was also puzzled by the meaning. Ann felt brave enough to ask a theological question.

"What happens to children when they die?" she asked.

"If they are very young, they go straight to heaven," he replied.

"How do you know this?" she inquired.

"The Bible says 'Let the little children come to me for such is the Kingdom of God.' In other words, the little children are a part of the Kingdom of God. They go straight to heaven as little children. They grow up there," he said.

Ann grew strangely quiet. Tears started to form in her eyes. Brian asked a very probing question. "Ann, did you lose a child?" She couldn't answer but the tears started flowing freely.

"I had an abortion. I tried to keep it a secret but it stills haunts me," she said, fighting the tears and wiping her face.

"Ann, abortion is forgivable. Jesus died so you could be free from your past. How long have you had to live with this?" he asked.

"Eighteen years. How could God forgive me? What I did to my own child? Now she is haunting me from the grave. If God loves me, why would I have these horrible dreams?" she asked.

"He loves you, Ann. Maybe this is the only way you will listen to him. Can I pray for you?" he asked.

"Ok," she said wiping her tears again.

"God, I pray that Ann would soon know and experience Your love. When she asks for forgiveness and receives your Son into her heart, I pray that she would know that she is free from her past. I pray that she would experience the fullness of joy that comes only from You. I pray this in Jesus' name, amen."

"Thanks," She replied. "Oh, I bet my husband is wondering where I am."

"Here's my phone number. Call me anytime you have a question or just want to talk. Also, here's the information about the church that I pastor here in town. Don't ever hesitate to reach me, OK?"

"I'll do that," Ann said.

She wandered back into the restaurant, deep in thought and a little dazed.

"Are you ok? You were gone a long time," John inquired.

"Yea, I'm ok," she said. "John…what do people do at church?" she asked.

"Well, I didn't think I would ever hear that question from you. Let's see. They sing songs, make announcements, take an offering, hear a sermon from the pastor, some places have communion. Why do you ask?" he asked.

"I was invited to a church by an old friend. I'm kind of interested in going some time," she said.

"Well let's do it this weekend. I haven't been to a church since I was a teenager. It will be fun going back," he said.

Going to church was a new experience for Ann. She expected priests in flowing robes haunting ornate cathedrals, chanting Latin masses. What she found was much different.

The church was small, the people happy and friendly. They greeted her as if she were an old friend. The whole scene took Ann by surprise.

Her husband John seemed like he was home again. Although the kindness and friendliness was strong, Ann still battled her fears.

Fortunately, the service started and she could focus on something other than new people getting to know her. She was still nervous and fidgety. Her husband tried to calm her. "Just Relax. They're not going to attack and eat you. That only happens at the Wednesday night service." he whispered. Ann cracked a little smile.

Her old principal came to the podium. He shared some announcements and introduced Ann and John. Ann did not want to be seen or heard. She quickly stood up and even faster, she sat down. She was getting embarrassed by all the attention as she shifted around in her seat.

The church sang a few songs. Pastor Brian introduced the guest speaker. It was a young woman whose life had come apart from guilt and sin. She shared her story about Christ coming into her life and how the burden of guilt which had felt like a weight had been lifted from her life. She talked about how good God was and how He helped her through the most difficult time in her life.

John turned to say something to Ann and noticed that she was crying. The message had struck a chord in her heart. It was the first time Ann had opened up her life to God. She went from crying to weeping. John put his arm around her. He was crying also.

At the end of the message, the guest speaker concluded with an invitation for prayer. John raised his hand, volunteering himself and Ann. They all met together and Ann poured her heart out to God. The guest speaker knew what she was going through because she had been through the same pain. They all prayed together and Ann's burden of guilt lifted. Even John felt a new peace. Their hearts had been made new right there in that small church.

That night Ann slept peacefully for the first time in years. She had no disturbing dreams. It was one of her best nights. Ann and John continued to go to that church and they grew in their faith. The people at her office started to notice a different boss. She was revealing a softer side of her personality that they never knew existed.

Chapter 7
Ann Gets a Surprise

On the way to work one day, Ann's car had a flat tire. She called John for help and waited by the car. As she looked, she could see a group of homeless people warming themselves at a ventilation duct. One of the men looked familiar and caught her eye. He gazed at her in recognition and quickly looked away. Ann continued to try to remember who he was.

John arrived. "I'll get this car fixed in a jiffy and get you back to work."

"John, That man over there. I know him from somewhere. I just can't place him," she told her husband.

"Be careful, honey. These people will rob you blind."

As she sat and pondered, a thought from nowhere penetrated her mind, *Go and ask him for a loan.*

Suddenly it occurred to her that the homeless man was Howard Stricker. He had been President of First Global Bank. He had gone through a divorce and lost his job due to heavy drinking.

Ann looked again. It was definitely him. She bolted out of the car and called after the shrinking figure. "Howard, Howard Stricker, is that you?" He stammered and started to run away. John looked on, confused. *Why is a homeless man running from a rich, beautiful woman?*

"Honey, what are you doing?" he asked as he got up from changing the tire.

"It's OK, John. Howard, please stop. I just want to talk," she shouted as she started to chase him. Howard continued to stagger away; being half drunk, he tripped and fell hard on his face. The fall started a nasal geyser of blood. Ann caught up to him as he lay injured from an obviously broken nose.

"Howard? Oh dear, you're hurt. John, call an ambulance. Howard is hurt," she shouted.

"No, No. I'm ok," Howard said.

"Howard, you're bleeding badly. You need a doctor," Ann insisted.

"No, I don't have any money. Leave me alone. I'm better off dead."

"Don't you dare say that to me," Ann snapped, the CEO firmly in charge. Howard knew from his time at First Global, not to cross her. He laid there and waited for the ambulance. Ann nursed his wounds and got the bleeding to stop. The ambulance arrived shortly after.

Ann called her office and told them there was an emergency and she would be in late. Ann rode in the ambulance while John took care of getting the cars back home.

Later, at the hospital, Ann got Howard to open up about his downfall.

"Ann, I couldn't deal with all the pressure at work. I found that a stiff drink helped me through the day. Then it became more and more. A drink, a pint, a fifth. My temper was out of control when I drank too much. After a horrible fight, I was kicked out of my home and had nowhere to go. Yet all I could think about was my next drink."

Howard paused, then looked into Ann's eyes. "How did you know who I was?"

"I saw the man in you," Ann replied, "The man I knew from work." She continued gazing at Howard long after he had dropped his gaze.

Ann vowed to help him. She paid for his hospital stay and enrolled him in rehabilitation. She even got him to go to church with her and John. Within months, God touched Howard just as He had touched them. One morning at church, Howard burst into tears. He prayed for Jesus to come and put the pieces of his life back together.

One morning, Ann woke up sick to her stomach. She stumbled to the bathroom, weak and nauseous, losing the best part of the previous night's dinner.

"Ann, are you ok in there?" her husband asked.

"I'm puking my guts out, for your information," she snapped.

He laughed, knowing that if she was that bad off, she would not have her sharp wit.

"I'll call the doctor," he answered while reaching for the phone.

"Why bother. It'll pass."

But her heaves got worse.

"Ann, get your clothes on," John informed her as he put down the phone. "You have an appointment in an hour." This time, there was no resistance from the CEO.

"John, what did you tell him to get him to get that appointment so fast? I hope you didn't get dramatic."

"That's for me to know and for you to find out," he replied, smiling warmly.

"You're enjoying my misery, aren't you? If this is deadly, I hope it's contagious," she shot back.

"I love it when you're mad. You're so cute." he said egging her on even more.

"Mad? You haven't seen mad. You haven't seen me mad yet but you are about to if you don't stop."

At the doctor's office, her physician examined her and didn't find anything. "Ann, you're going to have to come back to the office tomorrow. It doesn't seem to be serious. We are going to run some tests. Standard doctor routine."

"Ok, I guess I don't have a choice, do I?" Ann replied.

The next day, John and Ann received surprising news.

"Ann, we have the test results. Your health is fine, but you have a serious condition that should right itself in a few months."

Meeting her quizzical stare with a pregnant pause, the doctor added, "Ann, you are going to have a baby."

Ann gasped and turned to John. The doctor droned on, but he wasn't certain how much the blank-eyed couple was absorbing.

"Ann, here is some information on pregnancies late in life. Come back on this date and we'll do an ultrasound. Here's a prescription for pre-natal vitamins. Try not to work too hard. Also, you may be showing early signs of water build up. Be aware that there will be some risks associated with having a child at your age. If you want to discuss other options, I can arrange that for you," the doctor said.

"What options?" she asked.

"Well, I'm not really supposed to say," was the doctors contrite response.

"Don't give me that. Tell me what you are talking about or you'll be the one needing a stretcher," Ann declared.

"Ann, at your age, many women elect to abort their fetus for health reasons. You would be well justified if that is what you decide." The doctor stared at the floor.

"How could you say that? That's horrid. This conversation is over." Ann rapidly gathered her things and stormed from the room. John was equally angered. The doctor knew he had hit a nerve.

John and Ann continued their conversation in the car. "Why did he say that, John? Is this baby dangerous for me? Is something going to happen to the baby? I can't believe this is happening to me. I didn't even think I could have children. This is some kind of bad dream," she poured out.

"Ann, you're going to be fine. They give that standard line to everyone. There are plenty of women your age having children. Just think you'll be a mommy."

"I don't deserve to be a mommy, not after what I did to my first baby. This is just a curse for my past," she said as the tears formed.

"Don't say that. This is the greatest blessing you could ever get. I had a dream about a little boy just last night. I think it's a second chance for you and for us." Tears were forming in John's eyes as well.

"You know," said Ann. "If I had been pregnant before those dreams and before God came into my life, I would have had an abortion in a second. Maybe, just maybe, God is looking out for us and for the baby. It could be that everything happened to tell us what to do."

"That makes sense to me," John said as they smiled at each other.

Unfortunately, the board members and directors of Star Oil Company were less than enthusiastic when they found out about Ann's condition. Two days into merger discussions, the board held a secret meeting.

"We can't have her gone for 12 weeks. I can't believe she didn't have the sense to try to prevent this. What if she has complications? This company can't run this way."

The Chairman offered a solution. "What if we redefined her role in the company, or offered her a severance package?"

"Are you saying fire her? Out of the question," spoke the legal counsel. "That would spell lawsuit for sure."

"Maybe I could just talk her out of this baby nonsense," said the Chairman. "That would be the best option. I'm sure if she knew that the board was united in its feelings, it would be easy to sway her. It's the best thing for everyone, including her."

The board members nodded in agreement.

A week later, Ann was called into the chairman's office.

"Ann, how are you? Sit down for a minute," he said.

The atmosphere didn't feel right to Ann, not for a "let's get caught up" meeting. Her years as an executive had trained her to scope out any situation with her gut feelings and act accordingly.

Ann replied with unease in her voice, "My assistant didn't give me any details about why you wanted to talk. I have a tremendous amount of work to do today. I hope this is important."

He forced a relaxed reply, "It's just a friendly little chat. How are you coming with your new addition?"

"We are doing fine. Why do you ask? Charles, you are not usually concerned about my personal life. Why the new interest all of a sudden?"

"Yes, I know it is out of the ordinary. I just want to make sure you are doing ok. A pregnancy can take a toll on someone like yourself," he said looking for the right words as he pushed his short gray hair to the side.

"I hope you are not speaking from experience," she shot back.

"No, uh… Ann, I am concerned about the merger also. It's going to be a demanding time. I don't want anything to impact your health."

"What exactly are you saying, Charles?"

The chairman saw he had to be more straightforward. Ann was a straight shooter, and he would have to do likewise.

"Ann, you are important to this company, and you are important to me. I just don't want anything to put you at an unnecessary health risk. You know that there are medical procedures that can solve this… dilemma. Don't you think at your age, starting a family might not be the wisest thing right now? I'm sure you see my position on this. And frankly, the board agrees with me."

Ann seethed with rage.

"Keep your greedy hands off my baby or I'll break your neck. You tell the board that if my position is altered in anyway, they can expect a not-so-friendly call from my lawyer," she shouted as she stormed from his office.

Charles muttered to himself. *Well, that didn't go very well. Maybe she needs to be convinced in a different way.*

On the way home, Ann called her husband and told him everything that happened. "What is their problem? Do they think they own you?"

Her next call was to her lawyer.

"Ann, document everything. Be aware also that some corporate boards have put wiretaps on people's home and office phones to build a case against you. Be careful what you say and who you talk to. They can also blackmail you into quitting with a minimal severance package."

Ann had known many of the board members for years.

"Surely they wouldn't do something like that," she said. The lawyer's long silence told her otherwise.

Howard's recovery was going along well. His withdrawal symptoms were diminished. Better yet, he spent each day with God; his only solace in the storm of withdrawal and reconciliation. Today, he couldn't sit still, read the Bible, or even pray. All he could do was worry. A rehab worker saw his nervous pacing and called his counselor.

When the counselor knocked at the door, Howard hesitated to answer.

"Howard. It's Bill. Can I come in?"

Agitated and afraid, Howard acquiesced. Once in the room, the counselor asked Howard to sit down and relax. "Just a few questions, OK?"

"I don't feel very good. Can you come back tomorrow?" Howard said.

"Sorry, today is your appointment. I just came a little early. How are you feeling?" he asked.

"Confused, I guess. I don't know what to say. I don't know what to do. I wish I could say the right thing," Howard muttered.

What's bothering him today? With a jolt, the counselor remembered that Howard was meeting with his wife and children this afternoon. They hadn't seen him since he had left. It was going to be a difficult meeting. Howard had no way of explaining what happened to him or why he had fallen so hard.

"Howard, if you want to, we can give them the progress report and you won't have to say anything. But it is important that you see them. It helps their healing process as well as yours."

"I can't talk to them. I have screwed them over so bad," Howard said.

"Listen, you need to remember that God has forgiven you, so you need to forgive yourself. You're doing this to help your family heal as well." The counselor smiled with confidence.

"Yeah, I guess you're right," Howard said. "Hey doc, would you pray with me?"

Later the same night, a tall, attractive woman with dark hair approached the clinic meeting room with her two boys. They were 8 and 10 years old. They had not seen their dad for a long time. Questions swirled through their minds. The counselor greeted them at the door and gave them some instructions.

"Maggie, Don't argue. Don't show anger. It's ok to cry. You are free to hug him, however don't ask too many questions. He has been very nervous about meeting with you. He is deeply into the guilt and remorse part of the healing cycle. He loves you deeply and can't bear the pain he's caused everybody."

After the counselor left to get Howard, another counselor–looking slightly out of place—tapped on Maggie's shoulder, startling her.

"Tell Howard, the Lord says everything will be restored for him. God has a special plan for him and he will not fail or falter."

As Maggie struggled to absorbed this strange message, the counselor disappeared and the original counselor arrived.

"Are we all ready to go in?" he asked. Jubilant, the children yelled a resounding "Yay!" Maggie muttered a muffled ok. As the door opened, the kids ran toward their dad with arms in the air. They each grabbed a side and hugged him with all their might. Their joy overwhelmed Howard as he held them in return. He knelt down to be cheek to cheek with their unblemished faces. Their embrace squeezed an overflow of tears from their father's beaming eyes.

"Daddy, are you ok?" came the plea from an innocent face.

"I'm OK. I'm so happy to see you guys."

As his wife approached, Howard rose from holding his boys. There was an awkward silence as they looked at each other and gathered their emotions. His eyes continued to gush fluid, and tears covered his weary face. Maggie felt her own tears streaking her face. She leaned into him and they began a long embrace. What seemed an eternity was only a few seconds. His crying turned into heaving. He started to apologize for falling into the abyss—for taking them with him.

"I'm so sorry. What I did to you. What I did to the kids, what I…" His wife cut him off. Her memory of the strange counselor's words came back strong and clear.

"God is going to restore everything to you. He has a special plan for you and you will not fail," Maggie managed to say.

"I don't deserve this. I don't deserve any of this," he said with deepest regret.

"I love you and that's not going to change. You're coming back. Everything is coming back. You are not going to fall. Love will pick you back up," she said.

They continued to hold each other. After a long kiss goodbye, they pulled themselves away, knowing that their time was up, for now. The kids didn't go easily either. Maggie finally got the boys loaded into the car and drove away. Howard watched them from the rehab center's lobby as they faded from his gaze.

For Maggie, it was a quiet trip home. The kids fell into a sound sleep. Despite the gut wrenching emotion of the day, a smile remained on her face. She had a calm sense that the stranger's words were truth in the making, a heaven-sent prophesy of sorts. She relished the meaningful silence of deep assurance for the first time in a long while.

Meanwhile, Howard couldn't get her words out of his head. The warm feeling of embrace lingered in his room. His clothes still bore the weight of his children hanging from them.

Howard lay down on his bed and had the most peaceful sleep he had ever experienced. Although he was still in rehab, he felt something that he had never had, even at the peak of his success. He felt love's power. He felt God's presence. Its warmth filled every part of his empty soul. His mind could not wrap itself around the incredible peace abiding in the heart of a wrecked homeless alcoholic resting in a rehab bed. He realized without a doubt that his life had a higher purpose than himself. As he closed his eyes, he knew the same deep well of assurance that comforted Maggie on the other side of town, and they slept together for the first night in years.

The remaining time at rehab flew by like a supersonic jet, and Howard was finally ready to go home. But what home, he wondered. Despite the separation, Maggie allowed Howard to move back in with her and the boys. At this reunion, there would be no heart rending separation. There were no tears, but there were many hugs. Howard sat in the car with Maggie as she drove to the house. She felt a surprising sense of respect for this broken man who choose to rise from the ashes and love again. Her love for him took a new turn–stronger, more secure.

Within months, they were fully reunited and Howard started attending church with his family. He also started looking for a job. He did things around the house. He played tennis with the kids and helped with homework. He fixed supper in the evening and did the dishes while Maggie got some much needed rest.

A pleasant surprise rang through the telephone one day.

"Hello, this is Ann Wentworth. Is Howard there?" spoke the commanding and friendly voice.

"Ah, yes, he's right here," was Maggie's stunned reply as she handed the phone to Howard.

"Ann, I don't know how to thank you enough for finding me. I know my family thanks you. I would probably be dead right now if it wasn't for you," he said.

"Don't get all emotional with me. Rehab didn't make you go all soft, did it?" she shot back.

"Ann, how did you know where to find me? How did you even recognize me that day on the street?"

"Well, Howard, it's a long story." Ann shared with him her own transformation, starting with the dreams. She let it all out and spared no details. Soon they were laughing and crying together as they talked and prayed. Then she delivered the payload.

"Howard, I talked with some of your buddies at First Global Bank. I reminded them of how good of a customer Star Oil has been for them. They said they would take you back as a branch manager until you prove yourself. You know the routine."

"Yeah, and they couldn't say no to Ann Wentworth. Thank you Ann. I'll talk it over with the family. Who do I call if I say yes?"

She gave him the information and they said goodbye.

It wasn't long before Howard was back at work. To his surprise, people welcomed him back with open arms. They even threw him a party. It was difficult for him to not show emotion at the warmth. The other bankers noticed the subtle changes in him. He maintained his expertise and confidence but had a contagious kindness. Although his position as bank president had been filled, he quickly rose to vice president of risk management and internal auditing. The position interfaced with many different levels within the company. He soon became a business partner and friend to many people. Because of his brokenness, he gained new respect from his fellow employees.

About the time he was settled in his new position, he stumbled onto something that was too hot to handle by himself. He talked to his family and prayed for guidance, then he made a profound decision. One of his clients was getting large payments from a direct competitor of Star Oil. He started tracing the money trail. When he gathered enough information, he called the Securities and Exchange Commission as well as the Attorney General.

Some months later, Ann was greeted frostily by Charles Jenkins as she entered the boardroom for the regular board meeting. She was now seven months pregnant, and the animosity between her and the chairman had grown exponentially. The tension in the oak and cherry-lined room was palatable.

As she took her usual spot, the chairman started the meeting.

"The first order of business is the reassignment of officers. Up for vote is the new job assignment for Ann Wentworth to Vice President of Global Strategy. After which the vote on filling the dual position of Chairman and CEO, with myself. My administrative assistant will be passing out the voting forms."

Ann was stunned.

"What is this, Charles? A coup attempt. Who authorized this?" she shouted.

"Sorry you were not informed beforehand. Nevertheless, the vote must go on. Ann, let's not make this more painful than it needs to be. Many of us feel that new blood is needed. A fresh vision for the future. This is about Star Oil, not you. Sometimes, progress comes at a price."

Ann sat in silence. The old Ann would have ripped into them with ferocious temper. But today, a gentle whisper inside told her to wait calmly until justice arrived.

As the forms were being passed out, a wild ruckus sounded outside the board room doors. "Lisa, can you find out what is going on out there?" the Chairman asked. Before she could reach the doors, they burst open and legions of strangers filled the room.

"What is going here?" said the board members in layered unison. A broad portfolio from the Securities and Exchange Commission, Federal Agents, and City Policeman now occupied their sanctuary.

"Charles Jenkins, you are under arrest for Securities Fraud and Insider Trading. You have the right to remain silent. …," read the federal agent before they took him away. The board sat in stunned silence. They did not see this coming. Ann quickly filled the leadership vacuum. She knew the corporate bylaws gave her temporary control of the company in this situation.

With a determined smirk, she offered, "I make a motion that the vote for officer changes be put off indefinitely."

Without hesitation, the board agreed. After the shortened meeting, Ann got a call from her friend Howard.

"Ann, I hope you're not mad at me," Howard said.

"Why would I be mad at you?" she puzzled.

"Because I turned your boss into the police. I have been working on this for four months. It must have been a brutal surprise to have him arrested at the board meeting. That was the Fed's idea. I really didn't have any choice," he said.

Ann laughed and laughed. "Howard, God is so good. He works in wonderful ways. They were trying to get rid of me when the police came in. Let's have lunch tomorrow, I'll tell you all about it. Is the Waldorf at one-o'clock fine with you?" she asked.

"As long as you're paying."

"Sounds like a banker to me," she laughed.

Chapter 8
Charlie's Trip

As Charlie Harris finished high school, he felt called into ministry. His "Aunt" Beverly suggested he write a letter to her son David to see if they could use another hand in Ethiopia. David was ecstatic, sending Charlie information on developing support and applying to the missionary organization. Many of David's supporters were leery of adding Charlie, but they took David's word that Charlie would be a great help.

Charlie generated enough support to go, and finally got the letter from the missionary agency that he had been accepted. Before leaving, he visited his mother's grave For one last goodbye. At the gravesite, he started to tell about all of his struggles and pains, and how sad he was that he could not share his life with her. He reminded himself that he would be with her one day in heaven. He left the grave refreshed again. He wanted to see his mother so badly that he prayed, "God, if there is any way to see my mother again, let me tell her that I love her."

That night, as Charlie finished packing for his journey, he suddenly grew tired and fell asleep on the couch. In a dream, he saw his house burning as before. This time, however, he ran up the stairs looking for his mom. She wasn't anywhere to be found. He panicked and raced through the house.

When the smoke completely filled every room, he staggered out.

As he watched the house burn, he heard something behind him. He turned around to see his mother wearing a bright white robe. Charlie was so overwhelmed that he didn't know what to say. His mom hugged him And said, "God will be with you wherever you go, to protect you and guide you. You'll be with me very soon. I love you so much." As soon as she finished speaking, Charlie awoke from his dream.

"Thank you God," he said as he stretched back out on the couch.

In the middle of the night, Aunt Bev covered him with some blankets and sat beside him. She was filled with so many mixed emotions. She was sad that her time of taking care of Charlie had ended. But just because they were going to be thousands of miles apart didn't mean that she couldn't protect him in prayer. She was going to "cover" him in a very different way.

The next morning, Charlie arrived at the airport for his flight to Ethiopia. Charlie's luggage was checked in and he sat waiting to board the plane. He started to feel very strange about the flight, so he began to pray. When the time came for him to board, he felt a chill down his spine. He had not felt that way since he was a child. He asked God about going on this flight. He felt like the Lord was saying to be on your guard for evil men. Charlie started to back out but decided at the last second to board. He called "Aunt" Beverly and told her that he felt weird about the flight. Beverly prayed for him. Charlie took his seat in the front part of the coach section. He was being watched and he knew it. He continued to pray.

At home, Beverly continued to cover Charlie. "God, I pray that you would protect Charlie. Place your angels all around him that he would not be harmed. Give him wisdom, direction, guidance, and strength."

Suddenly, it was like the Holy Spirit took over her praying. The prayers took their effect as Hell's plans for the flight were stopped.

When Charlie landed in Addis Abbas, Ethiopia, there was excitement in the air. He had never been outside the US before. Everything was different. There were people everywhere, yet David was able to find him. Everything appeared to be in a state of chaos. Yet

WHEN DREAMS COLLIDE

David had done this routine many times. He knew every stop, every gate, and every danger.

David guided him in a hushed but firm tone. "Don't carry your money in your back pocket. Keep moving. Don't stare at anyone. We'll get out of here quickly and get to the compound."

Charlie felt nervous yet thrilled. He felt a strange warmth come over him. He knew he was supposed to be there. As they exited the airport, a van pulled up. Five Ethiopian men jumped out and whisked David, Charlie, and their belongings inside.

"You have good timing, brother," David said. The group greeted Charlie. Their English was limited but they showed their friendliness in a way that didn't require words.

"So, here is the one you spoke about. We will teach him to be an Ethiopian," one of the passengers said.

Charlie smiled. It was like a family reunion and he had just met his family for the first time. He was so thankful for Aunt Bev and David. They were his family, and now his family was growing rapidly. They rode for hours on rough dirt roads. The group spent the time praying, singing, and teaching Charlie how to speak Ethiopian.

Without warning, one of the group said something was wrong and everyone needed to pray. The atmosphere in the van quickly changed from joyful singing to a somber pray vigil. Charlie asked David, "What's going on?"

David answered, "Because of the dangers here in Ethiopia, prayer is a way of life. We remain sensitive to the Holy Spirit's call to pray. We have seen many times how, if we hadn't responded to the Spirit's nudge to pray, it would have been disastrous." Within minutes, the group was crying and moaning. The Spirit was interceding, praying through them and for them. This was a first for Charlie.

It continued for several minutes, until one of the group members started laughing and said in Ethiopian: "Brothers and Sisters, we have a release." The van erupted into singing and laughing. Charlie sat still in a state of confusion, though he felt the presence of God filling him and covering him with a strange and warm sensation just like in the airport.

After a few minutes, Charlie noticed a vehicle up ahead blocking the road. The group continued singing as if nothing was happening. The vehicle was filled with soldiers. Fortunately, they were government soldiers in search of a band of rebels. The van driver stopped, got out, and spoke with the soldiers.

The driver returned to the van with a smile. "He says there are reports of rebels in the area and he is going to escort us to the missionary compound." David relayed the message to Charlie in English. Charlie was relieved to know that this was a good encounter.

As the convoy started, one of the group in the van spoke out in Ethiopian, "Brothers and Sisters, the battle is not over. We must pray." Again, the mood inside the van took a wild swing. They continued the same routine as before. They eventually erupted back into song.

As they sped down the road, Charlie saw someone hiding behind a tree. He just had time to show David, when a bomb went off. The force from the blast sent the army jeep in front of them flying into the air. The soldiers in the army jeep were injured and stunned. The shockwave also broke the front window in the van. The driver stopped immediately.

Rebels swarmed from the forest and surrounded everyone. The soldiers could not get to their weapons in time. They had been ambushed. There seemed to be 50 or 60 heavily armed rebels. The group seemed to be unfazed by the encounter and continued their singing. Charlie was so scared that his legs were shaking. David steadied them. "It's ok. We're protected."

"Protected by whom?" said Charlie. "It can't be the soldiers. They are in worse shape than we are."

As the rebel leader approached the van, he stopped and waved them to go on. Ignoring the broken glass scattered across the dashboard, the van driver hit the gas pedal and sped off in a plume of blue smoke. No one dared even look back.

"What just happened?" Charlie asked.

"I don't know. I did tell you we'd be protected," David responded, "Charlie, I think you just saw the first of many miracles that you will see here in Ethiopia. We live by faith here. There's no other way."

Charlie sat back and pondered this. Later, he joined in the singing with everyone else.

An hour later, the van pulled into the compound. A few hundred people greeted them. David explained to Charlie, "These are mostly orphans and the elderly. Some are refugees from other areas where the fighting is bad. Some are blind, deaf, or crippled. The dying are brought here because there is no place else to go. The healthy ones grow vegetables and grain crops for the others. Other money comes from sponsors in the US and other countries.

The government is letting us use this land as long as we use it to help the people. We try to keep a low profile so we don't upset the rebel groups in the area. They see us as government spies, but don't have any proof. Receiving that government escort may be all the excuse they need to attack us now. It was God's provision or else our van would have been on top of that bomb. I can assure you our van would have been ripped apart by that blast. Here's your hut. You'll find everything you need. Dinner at six."

David continued, "Tonight, I'm going to introduce you to someone special. He's the spiritual elder here, a tribal chief of sorts. It won't take you long to figure out how unusual he is. He'll surprise you how much he knows about you. I haven't told him anything about you. The Holy Spirit shows him things about people. Don't be afraid of him. He's a very loving man. He'll encourage you but you can't hide anything from him. Also, he has a prayer shawl. Don't touch it. You'll know why later."

Charlie couldn't help feeling anxious about the evening. What was this man going to say to him? Charlie prayed quietly as he went to his tent. He tried to lie down for a nap but couldn't sleep. After lying awake, he decided to continue spending time in prayer, which grew rich and deep as the peace of God enveloped him. Meanwhile, in another hut, Demeke (the tribal elder) was speaking with David.

"Greetings David, I'm glad you brought him."

"I knew you'd know he was here. What do you sense so far?" David asked.

Demeke replied, "He is the one I have waited 15 years for. He will be severely tested very soon. But he will take my mantle and go all over the world." As he spoke, his voice cracked. Then he rose and danced around the room As David knelt and praised God.

Charlie arrived for dinner right on time. The food was plain and simple, but he enjoyed the variety of fruit. Many of the people around him could not speak English. They simply smiled and greeted their new guest. Their love could be felt in any language. Charlie still felt a pang of fear about the evening. He jumped when David came up behind and touched him on the shoulder.

"I'm sorry. I didn't mean to startle you," said David as he took a seat beside Charlie. "I'm taking you to Demeke's hut now, but I wanted to tell you more about him. When I came to this area, he was one of the first of the locals that I worked with. He is blind and when I found him, he was starving to death. He begged me to help him with some food. When I told him that I was going to build him a hut and take care of him, he started crying. He kept saying thank you in the Ethiopian language. As I learned to speak the language, I read the Bible to him. He cried for joy every night when he understood that God loved him. He prayed to receive Christ and later received the baptism of the Holy Spirit in a rich way. I read him the scripture that said, 'You will seek for me, and find me when you seek for me with all your heart.' He sought to meet with God for 40 days. He would only drink water. I was concerned after he became very thin."

David continued, "On the 40th day, an angel appeared to him and told him that his cry had been heard. The angel asked him what he wanted from the Lord. He said he wanted to see. The angel asked if he wanted to see in the natural or in the spirit. He said he wanted to see in the spirit. The angel picked up a prayer shawl that was in his hut and placed it on him. He said, 'You will now see into the spirit realm.

You will see all manner of angels, demons, and the condition of men's hearts. You will see if men are light or darkness. You will be given gifts of prophecy, wisdom, and knowledge. You will be a prophet of the Most High. When you are old, you will see with your natural eye and you will pass your ministry to another.' Charlie, all of the things the angel spoke have happened except the very last part. Don't be afraid of him. He will encourage you."

For some reason, David's words didn't make Charlie any less nervous as he slowly approached the hut with David. As they walked in, Demeke was standing at the other end of the circular room. He looked up in their direction and started speaking before being greeted, "Thank you, David. I wish to speak with Charlie alone."

"Of course," David said as he left the hut.

Charlie stood quietly.

"May I call you Charlie?" Demeke said.

"Yes, that's fine."

"Charlie, what is a piano?"

"It's a musical instrument. It has keys that move a hammer to hit a string." *Why would Demeke ask me about a piano? They don't even have pianos around here.*

Demeke asked, "Do you play the piano?"

"Not very well. I know a few songs."

"Charlie, I see you playing the piano in a place that will bring you great joy like you have never known. This word of prophecy will not make sense to you now. When it happens, you will know the Lord has spoken. There will be an attack tomorrow. They will target you. Don't be afraid. I have already prayed for your protection. I'm glad you're here. God spoke to me 15 years ago about your coming here. It is good to finally meet you. Your spirit light is strong but needs to grow. David and I will show you how. God has saved you from the fiery attack. I prayed for you then, just as I pray for you now. I know what happened to you as a child. Tell me Charlie, Have you forgiven your father for what he did to you and your mother?"

"I don't know. I try not to think about him," Charlie answered.

"You will need to forgive him and have a good heart towards him. The enemy has consumed him. It was through bitterness and fear that he opened the door to the enemy. The enemy has the same assignment for you. Never open that door to Satan. Be sure to forgive him."

Charlie suddenly felt faint and fell to the ground. When he awoke, he was in his hut, lying on his bed With no idea how long he had been there or how he got there. He barely remembered that he was in Ethiopia. He tried desperately to recall what Demeke told him. It started coming back to him: the piano, the attack, forgiving his father. All of it seemed so confusing and made no sense. Charlie started questioning why he was even there, so he started praying. He soon felt the presence of God in a very real way. He felt God reassuring him that he was in fact supposed to be there.

The next day, David spent all day with Charlie. David eventually asked him what Demeke said. "He asked if I played the piano. Isn't that the weirdest question? He said that I was going to be attacked today. He talked about my father," Charlie replied.

"What did he say about your father?" David asked.

"He asked if I had forgiven him. Honestly, I didn't know what to say. I don't remember much about him. All I can recall is when he killed my mother and tried to kill me. I just remember the look in his eye when he came at me. I am more afraid of him than angry at him. Sometimes, I close my eyes and see him chasing after me. I don't know that forgiveness has anything to do with me being here. Frankly, when you said those things about Demeke, I was expecting something different. He just didn't make any sense. I guess it doesn't have to. I just wish it did."

"I'm sure it will make sense soon," said David. "The piano part sure sounds odd. I know Demeke has a strong gifting and he has been incredibly accurate in what he knows. You're not disappointed that you came, are you?"

"No, No, I like it here. God keeps letting me know that I'm

supposed to be here. The drive here was unnerving. I hope I don't have to face those rebels again. I can't help thinking that they will be back."

David noticed a hint of fear in Charlie's voice.

"Why do you say that?" David inquired.

"I don't know. I just feel it. I guess that means that I should be praying about it," Charlie said.

"Let's do it now," David said. "Father, I just pray that the angels would surround the people in the compound tonight. I pray especially for Charlie's protection. I pray his faith would not fail when it is tested."

They continued in prayer. When one of them started to quit, the other one would feel compelled to continue.

After a while, they looked at each other and started laughing. They were so tickled that they couldn't stop. They didn't even know what they were laughing about. They were able to stop long enough to realize that it was time for dinner.

"Let's eat," Charlie said.

As they walked to the table, they walked by the front gate. They both stopped when they heard a twig snap.

"What was that?" Charlie asked.

"I don't know," David said. No sooner had David spoken, then five rebel soldiers jumped them. The soldiers tied their arms behind their backs. Soon, hundreds of soldiers surrounded the compound. The residents quietly stopped their dinner and sat still. It seemed surreal to Charlie. The people acted like they saw this every day.

The rebel leader, seeing the compound was secure, came out of hiding and approached David and Charlie. He had them taken to the center of the compound where everyone could see them.

He held a gun to David and yelled in Ethiopian, "Why have you brought the American spy? Why did you try to bring those soldiers with you to the compound? Are you wanting to set up a base? Are you wanting to kill us?"

David spoke in Ethiopian, "We're not trying to harm you. The soldiers just wanted to escort us. We had no choice. We've never harmed you before. Why would we start now?"

The rebel leader said, "Before we killed the soldiers, they said the American was a spy and they were starting an army base right here."

Before David replied, Charlie started laughing. It was unprovoked. He could barely control it. The rebel leader became furious. "Is this a game to you?" he asked. "This is what happens to anyone who opposes us," He yelled as he pointed his gun at Charlie and pulled the trigger.

The bullet struck Charlie in the temple.

But instead of killing him, the shot made Charlie laugh harder. The leader shot five more bullets into his head. The blood gushed from his scalp. Charlie never stopped laughing. The leader stood in amazement, watching Charlie. Everyone watched in stunned silence. The leader looked up to notice a tall, imposing figure before him. The figure slapped the leader so hard that he became airborne. He landed about 20 feet away, uninjured.

The whole compound, including some of the soldiers, started laughing. The leader became enraged. He got out his gun but it wouldn't reload. The soldiers, realizing what was happening, started to flee from the compound. Charlie and David were both on the ground laughing.

Demeke stepped out of his hut and approached the leader. "It is time for you to leave," he told him in Ethiopian. Fear enveloped the leader. He dropped his gun and disappeared in the darkness of the forest. All of the soldiers were gone within seconds.

The people from the compound rushed to David and Charlie. After untying them, they noticed that there were no bullet wounds, only blood. *It must have healed*, they reasoned. The laughter continued, becoming contagious and spreading through the compound.

The laughter incident started rumors throughout the region. Many of the local villagers started coming to the compound to see if the stories were true. The people retold the stories and prayed for the visitors. Many of the villagers were touched by the power of God. Many also decided to stay and learn all they could about God and the Bible.

Demeke and David spent months teaching and training the local villagers. Lives were transformed as great joy erupted in that place. The local rebels left the compound alone. A few of the rebels even quit their fighting and came to stay at the compound. Charlie learned Ethiopian and helped as he could. Everyone was amazed when, on one occasion, Charlie prayed for a blind man who received his sight.

Over the next few months, Charlie's life was transformed. One of the biggest miracles in his life was not the gunshots to the head, but forgiveness from the heart. He was able to start praying for his father. He started to feel love and not fear when he thought of him.

Demeke had known by the spirit that Charlie's bitterness toward his father was a big obstacle in his spiritual growth. That obstacle was now gone but another remained.

One night, Charlie started feeling afraid. It was almost overwhelming. He sneaked into Demeke's hut and fell asleep on his floor. It the middle of the night, Charlie rose up and noticed the hut was completely on fire. He ran over to Demeke but couldn't wake him.

He tried with everything he had but Demeke did not move. The roof and the walls were consumed in flames. The smoke was starting to choke him and he knew that he had to escape the flames without his friend. He glanced at the front door. Someone was jostling it. Charlie unlatched it. The door burst open, knocking him to the ground. A man walked in. The sight of him left Charlie breathless and paralyzed. It was his father. *How did he know I was here? Was he on the plane? How did he get here? This is impossible.* The smoke starting choking Charlie but didn't seem to affect his dad at all. An evil grin broke out on his face as he held the door open for another. His companion was a huge demon. It had horns and was covered with hair and muscles. Charlie tried to yell but no sound came out. He was doomed to die in that burning hut.

Without warning, Demeke rose up with a wooden staff in his hand and struck Charlie's father like Aunt Bev did years ago. His head twisted all of the way to his shoulder as the sound of breaking bones filled the smoky room. The demon cursed the name of God and disappeared, taking his father with him. Charlie regained his strength and ran to Demeke. Demeke was furious and yelled at Charlie, "Why did you open the door?" Charlie tried to explain, but he felt faint and collapsed.

He awoke sleeping in the same hut. Demeke was quietly praying. Charlie rose and hugged him. Demeke asked why. "Because you saved me from the fire last night," Charlie replied.

"I didn't save anyone last night. I slept all night. It looks like you snuck into my hut, though," Demeke replied.

Charlie was confused and described what had happened. Demeke told him it was all a dream. "Look at my hut, Charlie. Does it look like a fire was here?"

Charlie hung his head. "You're right. It was just a dream."

"No, Charlie. Not 'just' a dream. It meant something. Everything in your dream is a symbol. It was a message. Your father represented fear. Fear kept you paralyzed. My staff drove them out. The staff represented two things. First, it represented authority. Just like Moses' staff meant authority, so this staff in the dream meant authority. Second, its wood represented the cross of Christ. Charlie, you have authority in Christ to overcome your fear. That's what the dream is trying to tell you. You don't have to be afraid."

As time passed, Charlie grew stronger, and Demeke began to open up about deeper things.

"Charlie, can I tell you something?"

"Sure," Charlie said.

"I have never been to the ocean. I see it many times in my dreams. I want to feel the waves. I want to smell the salt water. I want to hear the rhythm of the waves."

Charlie offered to take him to the ocean even though it was four hours away and they had to cross into dangerous Somalia. Charlie asked David for permission. He had to think and pray about it. Demeke spoke with David privately the next day.

"It's time for this trip. You know it is," Demeke said.

"You can't go now. We need you. This compound is strong because of you," argued David.

"They are strong because of the Lord. Always remember that. They will grow even stronger without my help," Demeke reiterated. David was unconvinced. They continued their discussion for hours.

Charlie couldn't understand what all of the fuss was about. *For crying out loud, it's just a trip to the beach*, he thought. But he also knew David would not see things the same way.

David finally gave his consent for the beach trip, but only if Demeke would let the compound have a feast in his honor. Demeke did not like the idea, but agreed. The compound brought out their best clothes and their best food. Charlie had never seen this before. People came from many villages to honor Demeke, bringing the best Ethiopia had to offer. They brought musical instruments and played his favorite songs. They ate until they couldn't eat any more.

At the end, Demeke stood up and began to share about the Lord. He thanked David for introducing him to the Lord and the Bible. He shared some of his own struggles. He shared of his victories. He talked about the angel who had appeared to him. As he described the angel, Charlie realized that the same angel had been in his dreams. Then Demeke spoke with joy about Charlie–how he was to have him in his life, and how God spoke to him 15 years ago about a young man from America.

Charlie felt the same emotion choke him up. He could see the tears streaming down Demeke's face. He had really grown to love and respect this man.

Demeke continued to share about his visions of heaven and how beautiful it was. Everyone was deeply moved. Some felt Demeke was prophesying his earthly departure, and they started crying. Demeke told them to stop because heaven was such a happy place and that he was not afraid.

After the party, Demeke packed the things he needed for the trip. He called for David and Charlie to come.

"Charlie, I feel it is time that you learned how to use the prayer shawl. You will soon need it. Here put it on." Charlie didn't know what to expect. He wore it for a few minutes, but didn't see anything.

"I don't think it's working for me. There must something wrong with me," Charlie said.

This response frustrated Demeke.

"You must understand that every gift of God is unlocked with faith. Stop your foolish doubting."

"I'm sorry," said Charlie. But still, nothing happened.

"Voice what you want, Charlie," prodded Demeke.

"I want to see into the unknown realm. I want to see angels, demons, and the hearts of men. God, open my eyes," Charlie cried out.

Charlie closed his eyes as the Spirit's presence filled him to overflowing. Colors started to rise from darkness. It was as though he was looking through night vision goggles. Everything was a light green. Evil was a shade of black, and the good was white. Demeke and David were both a brilliant white. He looked at his own hand and saw that it was also white. He could see something black in the distance.

He reverently slid the shawl off his shoulders and into his shaking hands. "Faith works. This shawl is awesome." He now understood many of the things that Demeke had told him about the coming evil. It all started to make sense, understanding things at a new level.

The next day, they loaded the truck and left. Everyone seemed a bit too quiet for a big "vacation" to the beach. It seemed that the angels were travelling with them because there were no major run-ins with the rebels or any bandits. That alone was very different. The four hour trip flew by. Soon, they felt the warm humid breeze from the ocean. David knew the roads. They parked at the beach and set up their tents. David cooked some food as Demeke sat out by the water and took it all in.

"I have dreamed of this day," he told Charlie. As the sun started to go down, the most brilliant sunset was painted upon the sky.

I wish Demeke could see this, I wish he was not blind, Charlie thought to himself.

"Charlie, this is the most beautiful sunset I have ever imagined. The colors are so…radiant," Demeke said.

Charlie suddenly realized that Demeke's sight had been restored. What a glorious time to receive his sight. Charlie hugged his friend and they cried together.

David called that dinner was ready.

"I'll beat you there," Demeke said as he took off running to the table. David saw him running and could barely believe his eyes. They all sat down and thanked God for everything.

As they sat in the tent together, David fell asleep. The other two continued their conversation late into the night.

"What do you want to see next? Maybe you should see an American city with its great buildings or the mountains in Kenya," Charlie asked.

"I have seen the two things that I have always longed for," Demeke said.

"Well, I know you wanted to see the sunset. What else had you waited those many years to see?" Charlie inquired.

"Charlie, I wanted to see your face. I longed to meet you and give you everything I have. That was my dream. It stayed with me every day."

A lump formed in Charlie's throat. No one had ever valued him in that way. He didn't know how to respond. Here was a man who was everything spiritually that he wanted to be. It was like being an orphan your whole life and finally meeting a father that loved you since birth and you never knew it.

"I want to give you something. As David told you, an angel gave me this. I have always kept it. Don't let it out of your sight. Only wear it when the Spirit leads," Demeke said as he handed Charlie the prayer shawl.

"I couldn't accept this from you. You will need it more than me. I barely know how it works."

"No, I won't need it anymore," stated Demeke. Despite Charlie's objections, Demeke prevailed. Charlie accepted his new heavenly gift. The argument over, they both were soon fast asleep.

Late that night, a noise jarred Charlie awake. He couldn't see a thing. He was disoriented, and instinctively reached for the shawl. He could see everything in green. He saw the light coming from David as he slept but could see no light coming from Demeke.

He reached for his friend, only to feel his cold lifeless body. Stunned and confused, he sat down. *How could this be?* he thought. A light appeared outside the tent. He left to investigate. As he stepped out of the tent, he could see two lights. When he removed the shawl, he only saw a moonlit beach.

"God, open my eyes," he prayed with all his heart.

Without warning, they were both in front of him–Trojol and Demeke's spirit.

"Goodbye my friend. We will soon be together," Demeke whispered.

Suspended in time, Charlie could only watch as Demeke and the angel disappeared into the night sky. Charlie dropped to his knees and poured out his anguished soul to God.

Chapter 9
Jennifer Hill

Jennifer searched the mirror in vain for the beauty she once had. As she combed her long brown hair, she tried to ignore the bruises and welts left by her boyfriend's drunken rages. After running off with Roy at sixteen, her life fell apart fast. She didn't know he became abusive when he drank. She began using drugs to ease the pain. The grey flesh under eyes told her that she couldn't go on. Things had to change, and change quickly.

With sudden resolve, she grabbed a satchel, stuffed it with all her worldly possessions, and burst from the shabby apartment into blinding daylight. She had to get away before Roy knew she was gone. Her shaking hands made it hard to turn the key, but the car started with a lurch. She gassed it and headed for the highway, determined to run as far away as she could.

To calm her nerves as she sped down the road, she switched on the car's radio and began searching for her favorite song. When she looked back at the road, a truck was stopped in front of her. She swerved hard to miss it, lost control, and met an oncoming truck. It struck her with such force that the car flipped and spun several times.

Jennifer was thrown around the vehicle and knocked unconscious when her head crushed the windshield. The crumbled metal folded around her like a vise. As she came to, she realized that the car was upside down and gasoline was leaking on her. She could only scream as the vehicle burst into flames, covering her from head to toe with searing pain. She knew she was going to die and thought about her family—those who loved her—and could not bear to leave them.

"God, if you can give me another chance, I'll do what you want me to," she prayed.

At that moment, a fireman reached through the flames and pulled her from the wreckage. She was badly burned all over. He wrapped her in a blanket and laid her gently on the ground, telling her with a strong, assuring voice that she was going to make it. Through her haze, Jennifer noticed his outfit was purple. Stranger still, there was no ambulance or fire truck anywhere. She glanced over at her vehicle and could not understand how anybody could have survived. Overwhelmed with pain, she passed out again.

As the firemen, paramedics, and police arrived, they were surprised to find Jennifer out of her car. Since she was unconscious, they couldn't ask her any questions as they applied first aid. The truck drivers told the police about the fireman who pulled her out of the wreckage.

The police did not believe them. "The doors are smashed shut. The roof is crushed. No way anybody got her out of there. There must be another vehicle somewhere."

But the truckers were emphatic. "The fireman came out of nowhere. He jumped in the middle of the flames. He was there in less than a minute of the accident."

Still, the police remained unconvinced. "The closest fire station is at least ten miles away in Bradford. Unless he was a good-Samaritan driving by. Even so, how could he…?"

The truckers started to get upset. "Don't call us liars. We know what we saw."

"OK, OK. I'll take your statements," the policeman said. "We'll be asking the girl what happened too…if she lives."

Jennifer woke a day later in a clean, white hospital bed. Even though she was still alive, she couldn't help but fear for her future. Her face, hands, neck, and torso had been badly burned in the fiery crash. Her pain slipped into despair as the reality of her plight grew.

In the coming days, doctor after doctor came to see her and offer their plans for her healing. Skin graph operations were scheduled. Bandages were changed constantly. The pain was unbearable, even with medication. The hospital staff tried to help. They knew the agony that she was going through. The caring staff was a small ray of sunshine for her, but they couldn't stop the flood of dark emotions Jennifer was drowning in.

One evening, a man dressed in scrubs walked down the hall toward Jennifer's room. The staff assumed he was a visiting resident and left him alone. Entering her room, he pushed back the curtain and sat next to her bed.

"You seem to be making progress in your recovery, Miss Hill."

Jennifer sat up in her bed. She was angry at the world and in no mood for another visitor with another plan, offering more false hope. She knew her situation was dire, and she wanted to be left alone to deal with it.

"Why can't you people just let me die," she said sullenly.

"Miss Hill, your life was spared for a reason," he calmly responded.

"Life! What life? I might as well be dead. No one will love this ugly, mangled piece of death. Look at me!"

"Miss Hill, people will love you more than you know. New people in your life will accept you. You have a wonderful future. I have seen it. Oh, and one more thing: you are beautiful."

This was the last straw for Jennifer. "I'm not beautiful! You're crazy," she screamed.

"Jennifer, I am not a doctor. I was sent here to remind you that you are God's workmanship—his creative masterpiece. He made you and he loves you completely. That will never change. He is always with you. You will never have to be afraid. I have one instruction for you. As you look in the mirror every day, thank God that you are beautiful."

"Who are you?" Jennifer demanded.

"Who I am doesn't matter right now. You can call me Trojol. What matters is that God loves you. You'll learn more about me later."

Jennifer's attention was abruptly distracted by something falling from her shelf. She glanced over to see a flower vase smashed on the ground. She turned back to ask the visitor for help, but he was gone. Yet, there had been no footsteps. *He couldn't run out that fast,* she thought. She looked back on the mess and saw the vase back on the shelf as if it had never fallen. She sat in stunned silence.

Who was that man? Not knowing what else to do, she rang for the nurse.

"Yes, can I help you?" was the reply from the intercom.

"Can you come in here? I need you for a second," Jennifer asked.

"Sure Missy. I'll be right there," the voice replied. The nurse arrived in seconds. "What do you need, Missy?"

Jennifer did not know what to ask for. After a few awkward moments, she finally asked, "There was a man here in my room. Was he a chaplain or something?"

"Missy, we don't have a chaplain on duty tonight. What did he look like? Do you know his name?"

"His name was Trojol. He was tall. He had short curly dark hair. He looked young, but he wasn't. I'm not sure."

"Well, Missy, I'll check around."

After the nurse left, Jennifer tried to remember what the visitor said. *There was something about a mirror. He wanted me to say something when I'm looking in the mirror. Oh, yeah! I'm supposed to say 'I'm beautiful.'*

A few minutes later, the nurse returned. "Missy, no one knows anyone named Trojol. And no one matches that description. Are you sure you're ok?"

"Yeah, I'm fine. Guess I was imagining it all. It's OK."

The nurse left the room puzzled and concerned.

Why did I react like that? Jennifer thought. *How did he know the perfect things to say? How did he get out of that room so fast?* All of a sudden it hit her: Trojol was an angel. He was sent by God.

A tear trickled down her scarred cheek. God had answered her prayer. She rang the nurse again.

"Nurse, can you bring me a mirror?" she asked.

"Uh, Missy, I don't think that's a good idea. The doctors, they don't like patients to… Why don't you try to get some rest," she objected.

"It's fine. I'm OK. I just need a mirror," Jennifer insisted.

The nurse came in with a sedative, insisting that Jennifer take it before laying a small mirror by her bed.

Jennifer's eyelids grew heavy. She fell asleep and slipped into a dream. She found herself backstage at some type of theater. There were props, ropes, costumes, and a back wall leading to a rear exit. It was dark but she could still see her way around.

A loud banging came from the rear exit door. Someone or something was trying to get in. Instinctively, Jennifer tried to run from the door but got tangled in the ropes on the floor.

The door burst open, revealing a ghoulish-looking man dressed in black, his face a ghastly grey. He held a noose in one hand and razor blades in the other. Jennifer could see something written on his forehead. She could only make out the letters S-U-I. The rest were covered by his dark, matted hair.

The man saw Jennifer struggling, and he screamed so loud it shot right through her. She tried to run again, but all of her energy was gone. She cried out to God in her terror, and the ropes loosen from her ankles. She was able to start moving away from the man but he was much faster. As he overtook her, he spoke through his blackened smile, "Jennifer, you will be mine this very night."

"No," she yelled as she struggled to escape.

Without warning, a spotlight came on, illuminating an area 10 feet in front of her. In the light, she saw something to fight with—a mirror and a sword. They must have been props for a play, she reasoned. As she struggled to reached the sword, the man closed in on her, his fetid breath mingling with her panicked gasps.

She reached the sword and swung at him, feeling her strength return. As he recoiled to avoid the blow, she saw the rest of the phrase on his forehead: SUICIDE. She swung the sword again and this time it cut him. He hesitated for a moment and laughed.

"You are mine. You cannot resist. I am the only one who wants your mangled form. You are useless to everyone but me."

With a cracked voice but firm resolve, Jennifer countered with these words: "I'm beautiful. I'm beautiful. God made me beautiful."

The man broke out into derisive laughter. "You are a useless rag. God is punishing you. No one loves you. No one wants you. I am stronger than you and you know it. I will win this very night."

Jennifer felt the power of his words, but sensed growing strength in her own. "No, No, No, you won't."

She swung the sword, harder this time, and the man winced in pain. Then he smiled, seeming to relish it.

"You can't overthrow me. I have killed millions just like you. I am your future. You are mine forever. It's time to join the others."

"I'm beautiful. I'm valuable. I'm loved. You are my enemy," she shouted as she swung again. This time the man seemed truly dismayed at her behavior. She was drawing strength from the light and the sword. He lunged at her but she swung with everything she had. As the blade cut an arc through the charged air, strong hands joined Jennifer's and increased the sword's power tenfold, striking the man so hard that he flew into the back wall, his bones cracking on impact. The building shook.

Incredibly, the man stood up and shouted, "I'll be back when you are weak again." He slipped out the rear exit and into the swallowing darkness.

Jennifer turned to see who had helped her. She saw a large man dressed in white, arrayed in dazzling glory. "Here, follow me. You are to go this way," he said as he took her by the hand. She quickly followed him through a maze of curtains, the light in the theater increasing as they moved.

One curtain remained. The one in white told her, "When you walk through this curtain, the Holy Spirit will show you what to do and what to say." She heard voices on the other side. The one in white pulled the curtain back. Jennifer found herself on stage behind a podium and a microphone, before an audience that gasped as she started to speak. With her first words, the people burst into a standing ovation.

She woke up from her dream. She was still in her hospital bed.

"It was a dream," she said, amazed at how real it seemed. She saw the mirror left by the nurse, and reached for it, but it vanished.

She realized that the dream was from God, to show her the way out of her sorrow and how to fight suicidal thoughts. She began to speak the words of God brought by the heavenly messenger: I am beautiful. I am loved. I have value.

That day was the beginning of recovery for Jennifer Hill. Even though she had been badly burned almost everywhere, including her face, she fought back by declaring her inner beauty and value. She started to see not only herself but others through different eyes. She started to see people for who they really were and not how they looked.

After a month in the hospital, the doctors told her that she was well enough to leave. Before she left, she visited the other burn victims, telling them how beautiful or handsome they were. She would tell them about God's great love for them. Many were angry and bitter just as she had been. Others were touched by her kindness, knowing that she had been where they were and had not only survived but was thriving.

One day, a man came to the hospital and asked to visit her. "Hi, my name is Dale Smith. I am looking for Jennifer Hill."

"I'm Jennifer Hill. Can I help you?"

"I was driving in the area and I felt like God wanted me to come to this hospital and pray for you. He told me your name," he said sheepishly, not knowing how she would react.

"Well, what are you waiting for?" she said, putting him at ease.

Dale gently put his hands on her bandages and spoke firmly: "By the stripes of Jesus Christ, you are healed."

Jennifer had never heard anyone pray that way before.

"Yes, Lord, I receive it," she said, assuming that the prayer was for her heart to be healed from the drama of the last few months.

"Well, Jennifer, I sure felt something. I guess I'd better be going now. Thank you for not thinking that I am crazy," he said.

"Thank you for the prayer."

That was very nice, she thought to herself.

The next morning, she dressed and walked to the hospital snack bar. Her morning routine included greeting Gladys at the counter. Even though the burns had grossly disfigured Jennifer, Gladys always greeted her by saying she was beautiful. Jennifer had started it and there was now a de-facto game of who would be first to tell the other they were beautiful. But things were different this morning. Gladys was not at the counter this morning. A young Hispanic man waited for her order. Because the beauty game had been going back and forth, Jennifer decided to say something to the young man.

"You are looking handsome today," she said. He blushed and hesitated to say anything. Jennifer thought to herself, *I guess I was out of line. He's probably never seen anyone scarred like me. I hope he's not offended.*

"Senorita, your face is the most beautiful face I have ever seen. It is truly angelic," he said.

It shocked Jennifer he was able to see past the scars and give her such a compliment.

"Thank you. That was very kind," Jennifer said.

Gladys was in the back making a tray of biscuits, and stepped out when she heard Jennifer's voice. As Gladys looked at Jennifer, she froze, dropped the pan of biscuits, and screamed. Jennifer thought that

WHEN DREAMS COLLIDE

something was happening behind her and turned to see why Gladys had screamed. Gladys ran to Jennifer as she turned back around. "Your face, your face...," Gladys kept repeating.

"Gladys, what's the matter? You know what I look like. Why are you acting like this?"

"Someone get me a mirror," Gladys yelled.

Jennifer wanted to run but before she could, a woman pulled out a compact mirror. Gladys gave it to Jennifer and told her to look. By then everyone in the snack bar was staring at them.

Jennifer had not looked herself for a week. *Have my scars gotten worse?* She opened the compact and saw herself. The compact dropped to the floor. The face she saw was perfectly normal. No scars. It was a mistake. Or had she been healed? Hospital security had been called because of the screaming. They all knew Jennifer and stared when they saw her.

Time froze. A snapshot lingered for an eternity, broken by a security worker radioing his fellow comrades. "Guys, come to the snack bar. You have got to see this."

Within minutes, not only had the entire security team showed up, but all of the staff in the burn unit and many of the patients as well. People hovered around Jennifer, touching her face.

"It's a miracle. When did this happen?" people asked. Jennifer didn't know how to respond. She didn't know exactly when it had happened. She was just as amazed as everyone else. Jennifer realized that God had touched her and he was now calling her to a life that she had never dreamed possible. She spent the rest of that day sharing about Christ's love with others and praying for the other burn patients. The hospital would never be the same. Even the hardest hearts were softened by the miraculous display of God's love and power in that place.

Two weeks later, she was out of the hospital and invited to a high school to speak about her experiences as a burn victim. She entered the back of auditorium and realized that the props, the ropes, the curtains, even the brick wall in the back, were all in her dream. As she stepped past the curtain and walked to the podium, the entire student body rose to their feet in thunderous applause.

She could not hold back the tears, remembering how she had fought the thoughts of suicide. God had given her glimpses of her future as he prepared her for this day. As she paused at the microphone for the applause to subside, a clear voice passed through her mind: "The Holy Spirit will show you what to do and what to say."

Gathering her breath before the rapt audience, she spoke in clear and measured tones.

"No one can say that things can't be turned around. There is no one without value in God's eyes. He can change everything in an instant and it will remain changed forever. Men look on the outside. They don't see as God sees. What may be ugly, fat, short, deformed, dumb, crippled, or useless to man, is beautiful, valuable, strong, powerful, and desirable to God. He makes all things new. He removes the guilt, pain, shame, hate, and darkness from your life and fills you with his light and glory, his love and value.

Two months ago, my life was filled with such darkness that I thought suicide was my only option for dealing with the pain of severe disfigurement. Was I ever wrong! God told me to call myself 'beautiful' and 'valuable,' regardless of what I looked like. And he was right, of course. Then he even surprised me by healing me. By seeing myself through His eyes, my heart became healed. I was able to reach out and help others in my same situation. But God is always one step ahead of us. I had completely accepted my circumstances, but God obviously had other plans.

If you don't like yourself, start telling yourself how much God values you. He made you with a special plan in mind, a plan that only you can fulfill, no one else."

The thunderous applause echoed the deep impact her words had on these students as they returned to their everyday world.

After her healing, Jennifer's heart for the people in the burn unit only grew deeper. Due to the notoriety of her story, the hospital offered her a position as a patient care representative. She would get to talk and pray with patients and their families all day. She spent most of her time in the burn unit.

One situation proved most challenging–a middle aged man who was the sole survivor in a house fire. The fire had taken the lives of his wife and two young daughters. The man's burns were not life threatening but his emotional state was very volatile. He would neither sleep nor cry. The doctors loaded him up with a host of medications both to ease his pain and reduce his mental anguish.

Jennifer was there to help. She spent a couple of days praying for the man before she ever approached him. At the prompting of one of the doctors who was seeing his condition worsen, she decided to talk with him.

"Knock, Knock," she said as she opened the door. "Are you decent?" she asked. There was no reply. She started to ease into the room. The man was lying on his back in the bed. He was awake but not interested in doing anything but staring at the ceiling.

"Hey, I know you probably don't feel like talking but I'm Jennifer. I'm your patient care representative. I'm here to find out if you are doing ok and make sure the hospital is helping you. I noticed that you have a beautiful vase of flowers by your bed. Did someone get them for you?"

The man continued to stare. Jennifer read aloud the note on the vase: "'You are in our prayers. From the members of First Community Church.' That's nice of them. Have they had a chance to visit you?"

Again, silence, but his eyes weren't focused on the ceiling anymore. He was looking straight at Jennifer. She could tell he had been crying. His eyes were puffy and red, and his nose was running. He hadn't shaved in weeks.

Jennifer looked on his name tag. "Jeff Ellison. Can I call you Jeff?"

No reply.

"Jeff, I know that you probably won't believe this, but I was a patient here in this same unit. I thought my life was over. But some people reached out and prayed for me, and my life turned around. I want you to know that I am praying for you. That's it. Good night." Jennifer walked toward the door.

"Don't bother," Jeff mumbled as he went back to staring at the ceiling.

"I'm sorry. I didn't hear what you said," Jennifer answered.

"I said, don't bother praying for me. You're wasting your time."

"Why do you say that?"

"Because, I won't be here tomorrow. I'll be in the morgue. I don't deserve to live. I killed my wife and kids. Did you read the report? I was drunk, passed out on the couch. A cigarette caught the couch on fire. My wife got me out of the house but died trying to get the girls out. She had been begging me to quit drinking and stop smoking. She begged me to go to church with her but I never would. It's my fault. What did they do to deserve this? Tell me that. Why did God kill the good and let the scum live? I don't deserve to live. I should've died in that house. I'm gonna die now."

"Jeff, I didn't know all that. I can't imagine your pain right now. I do know that God loves you and wanted you to live. I don't know why your family died, but I know one thing. Your family loved you. What would be the one thing you could do to honor your family? What's one way to show them you loved them? They wouldn't want you to hurt yourself. They would want you to be happy and start doing the right things. What would they say to you if they were right here?"

"They would hug me," sobbed Jeff, "and say that they love me. They always…" Jeff broke down and couldn't speak further.

"Well, now you have something to think about as you go to sleep tonight," Jennifer said as she left. "And I'll pray for you."

Jeff sobbed a while longer, then closed his eyes in a peace he had not felt since the accident. He fell asleep quickly and, hours later, began to dream.

Fog was everywhere. He was tied down with enormous chains from which he struggled to break free. He could hear his wife's voice calling for him, but he was too exhausted to call back. He could not even mutter a call for help. In seconds, his wife appeared, dressed in white. A figure that Jeff knew to be Jesus stood with her. She held a golden key which she used to unlock the chains. Jeff broke loose as his wife and Jesus smiled. Jeff heard his children playing in the background. His wife reached out to touch him and he woke with a start.

Jeff realized it was just a dream, but he still ached for her touch. He could not forget the love in Jesus' eyes. He reached for the card with the flower vase. He thought for a moment and had an idea, climbing back into the bed with a hint of resolve on his damaged face. "Tomorrow is going to be a new day for me."

Chapter 10
David and Charlie Come Home

Charlie and David were subdued as the plane landed in Louisville, Kentucky. They rented a car and drove to Sharpsville. Charlie was anxious to see Aunt Bev—he had so many things to tell her of the past three years. David couldn't wait to see his Mom.

As David pulled in the driveway, all of his childhood memories came pouring in. Charlie was reliving his childhood here too.

When Bev came out to meet them, they saw that she was a little slower and had lost weight. "Mom…you OK?" David asked as he approached.

"Well, aren't you going to hug your mother?" she joked, accepting his arms and starting to cry. "I have been praying for just one more chance to hold you. I love you. Please tell me you'll be here awhile," she said.

"Don't worry. We're staying as long as you need us," David replied.

Then her eye caught Charlie standing off to the side. "Charlie, is that you? Come here and hug your Aunt Bev," she said, not letting go of David.

"It's group hug time," Charlie said as they all embraced. Before long, they were seated around the dinner table enjoying one of Bev's great meals.

"Mom, we're going to Thomasville Community Church tomorrow to speak about our missionary work and raise some support. I hope they enjoy our stories of miracles," David said.

"I've heard some bad things about their pastor. Don't be surprised if you don't receive a hardy welcome. He may not like your stories. He tried to kick some people out of their church because they said they got healed after prayer time last week," Bev said.

"Well Mom, they support us, so I need to speak and let the donors know what they are giving to. I've been in some worse places before and I haven't got killed yet," David added.

"I hope you know what you are in for," Bev replied.

Later that night in the same town, a single mom named Mary fought with her autistic son, Mark. He had become agitated about the way she had made the bed. He screamed and toppled a tall bookshelf in anger. Mark had become too violent for her to handle. In her desperation, she cried, "God, I need your help. You know that this is too much for me. I need you to do something."

Mary collapsed on her bed and drifted into unplanned sleep. In the middle of the night, she woke suddenly and rushed to Mark's room, worried that he may have harmed himself. She was relieved to find him sleeping in his bed. As she watched his slumber, he suddenly woke and talked to her.

"Mom, I had a dream that there was a big present for me at church. I opened it and heard people saying 'Glory to God!' Why did I have this dream, mom?"

"I don't know. Can you go back to sleep now?" she said.

"OK," he said, slipping back into sleep.

I guess I'll get to that book shelf tomorrow after church, thought Mary as she headed back to bed.

The next morning, Charlie and David got dressed and ready for church. David told his friend, "I have a bad feeling about today."

Charlie replied, "It's God's day. If He shows up, who cares what happens." However, David did not share his positive view of the visit.

One thing they did agree on, however, was a strong urge to pray beforehand. They began to feel that something powerful was going to happen soon.

Mary woke up late for church. She broke the news to Mark that they weren't going because they were too late. To her surprise, he started throwing things and screaming, "My present, My present, My present."

"What are you talking about?" she cried in anguish.

It had been a long journey for Mary and Mark. His father had divorced her two years previous due to the strains of raising a difficult child. She maintained care for him with little to no help, and her nerves remained stretched very thin most of the time.

As Mark's tirade continued, Mary whispered a desperate prayer, "God, I can't do this anymore. Please God, just help me make it through today. Find him a good home without me." Mary had to face the facts: her job as caregiver was ending.

Mark continued screaming, oblivious to Mary's emotional breakdown. As she wondered where to turn, a thought came to her. *Just go to church late.* For some reason, this thought carried a power to get it done.

Mary's tears dried up as she gathered her resolve once more. "Ok, I guess we will go to church today. Get ready," she shouted.

Mark stopped his rampage and got dressed immediately. Before she could gather her things, he was in the front seat waiting, rocking back and forth in the car.

Well, I guess I have one less thing to worry about. Why was he talking about a present? She had forgotten the dream and assumed there was some kind of children's church give away where they had promised him something. The church had been a big help to her recently and it was greatly appreciated.

David and Charlie arrived at the church, stumbled upon a prayer meeting, and quietly joined in. "God, we pray that you would pour out your power in this place and do miracles. You are a God of the miraculous and we pray your wonders would be revealed in this church. Manifest your glory," the leader prayed.

Just then, a door slammed open, an irate man came in, and starting shouting at the prayer group leader. "If I have told you once, I have told you a thousand times, stop praying for the miraculous. Everyone knows that miracles do not happen in this day and age. This prayer meeting is not scriptural and I won't allow it to go on in this church."

The prayer group leader squared her shoulders and replied, "You can't stop us from praying, and you won't stop God from doing miracles in this place."

"If there is a miracle here, it will be from the Devil because he will be using your rebellious prayer meeting," the man retorted as he stormed out.

"Who was that?" David asked.

"He's our new pastor. The denomination sent him to 'fix' this church. I figure he'll be gone in a couple of months. The denomination has tried this about three times. They own the building so I guess they just keep trying. We just keep praying. I hope this didn't scare you from coming back. By the way, my name is Sheila. What's yours?" the leader asked with a peaceful smile.

"I'm David Parker and this is Charlie Harris. We are the missionaries that your church supports."

"We are so pleased to meet you. We pray regularly for you," said Shelia. "Tell us about your work."

David then shared story after story of God's power and faithfulness on the mission field. He thought, *the pastor may not appreciate these stories. I'll have to show some discretion in the service.*

After the prayer meeting, Charlie pulled David aside. "I had a powerful dream that God was going to do some mighty things in service today."

This put a huge lump in David's throat. *There goes our financial support. I guess it's back to selling cars for this ex-missionary,* he thought.

"Charlie, why don't you start it off during the sermon time? That way I can escape before it gets ugly," David said.

Charlie caught on to his humor and said, "I would love to start. Are you going to provide cover when the shots get fired?"

"I'm behind you all the way, way behind you," David said, laughing as they made their way to the sanctuary.

The sanctuary filled with people from all walks of life. Rich, poor, old, and young filled the seats. Introductions were made and the worship started. The songs were rich and emotional as everyone sang heart-felt praises. David and Charlie felt an unusually strong presence of the Lord in that place. They looked at other, smiled, and nodded in agreement. "Oh, yeah."

Some people were kneeling, some were crying, and others were smiling. After putting on his prayer shawl, Charlie glanced at the podium and had to readjust his focus. He could not believe what he was seeing.

Trojol was standing at the front and was placing a large golden bowl on a stand, filled with some kind of oil. The bowl was beautiful, covered with jewels of many different colors. Trojol motioned for Charlie to be silent about his presence. Charlie stayed in a quiet attitude of worship.

As all of this was happening, Mary pulled into the church parking lot with her son. Before the car had come to a complete stop, Mark bolted out of the car. She parked and ran in after him. Try as she may, she could not keep up with him. Mark ran into the sanctuary and saw the golden bowl at the altar. To him, it appeared to be a large wrapped present. He picked up his stride, running full steam toward his "present." He outran the ushers, then tripped and fell into the podium with a crash.

Charlie saw the bowl fly into the air and come crashing down on the boy. Charlie looked at Trojol to see if judgment would fall on the boy for being irreverent. Instead of looking stern, Trojol was rolling on the floor laughing. *Was this a time to be laughing?* Charlie thought. When he looked back at the sprawled form of Mark, he saw oil miraculously covering the dazed boy. The entire congregation saw it too, but they didn't see what the oil was doing on the inside. Mark's autism was being healed.

The pastor was enraged with the disruption and hastened over to boy as if to remove him. Two angels intercepted his stride and knocked him to the floor. They took flaming swords and pierced his head and hands. He grimaced in pain, not knowing that three holy swords were sticking out of him. Mary ran into the sanctuary just in time to see the spectacle. She ran to Mark, who also did not understand what was happening to him. Then he started feeling different, as if every thought, every emotion, even his perceptions and outlook, were changing.

Mary watched in awe as the son she always knew, emerged from Mark. She embraced him. And for the first time in his life, Mark understood the emotional warmth of her embrace. Mary felt the change and could not let go of her son. The ushers rushed to help the pastor, allowing Mark and his mom to relish God's beautiful restoration. The angels removed the swords.

"Now, every time your hands start to burn, you must heal the sick," the healing angel told the pastor. His hands felt as though they were dipped in acid.

The pastor understood his directive, calling out in a shaken voice:

"If there is anyone sick, I need to pray for you right now. Come up front."

Sheila couldn't believe her ears and neither could the prayer group members. The pastor prayed for at least a hundred people that morning, seeing numerous miracles. He kept laughing and crying throughout the morning, laughing that God had chosen him of all people, and crying that he had been shown such mercy. The church burst into song for hours. After the service, the deacon board let David know that he would be fully-funded for as long as he stayed on the mission field.

Charlie chuckled and said, "I never got to say a word."

"It was your best sermon ever," David replied.

Chapter 11
Tom and Charlie Reunite

One night, Tom had a dream. He saw the remains of a battle. Destruction was all around the battlefield and the sky was dark. Everything was murky and gray; nothing was alive, not even the grass. He breathed in the smells—pungent and rotten. He grimaced from the pain and sorrow which must have transpired here. He felt the anguish of every death, every pain, every disappointment, every fear, every injustice. He writhed in agony.

Thousands of voices cried, screamed, and ultimately died here. As he closed his eyes, unable to bear it, someone touched his hand. A strange warmth flowed from this person. Tom's pain started to subside as strength filled him. The man spoke in a whisper, "You have felt my pain, now feel my power."

The flow of liquid warmth gave way to a high voltage jolt of electricity. Light coursed through every fiber of Tom's being. He stumbled through the maze of death that was once a battlefield. Only now, everything he touched came to life. Dried branches grew leaves, and rotting flesh became healthy and whole. Where moans of pain had been, laughter now filled the air. Everything battered and scarred turned to beauty. Every horrid smell turned to a sweet perfume. The thousands of dead were now alive and filled with joy. Smiles broke out on every face as the light was coming from all directions and leaving no shadows.

Tom's heart cried out, "How can this be?"

The whispering man said, "I will show you the way."

He was jolted from the dream by someone shaking him.

"Tom, wake up."

Still half asleep, Tom retorted, "Leave me alone!"

It was Bill. "I thought I saw someone in the house. It must be a burglar. I'm going to look around."

Tom readjusted his focus, turned on the light and saw no one there.

Bill came back from scouring the whole house. "I guess it was just a false alarm. I'm sorry that I woke you. I would have let you sleep if I felt it was safe. You were talking heavily. It must have been some dream."

"Did I say anything interesting?" Tom asked.

"No, not really. It was mostly mumbling."

"Well, I'm going back to my dreams now," Tom said groggily. "Don't wake me up next time. Oh, wait Bill, you left your note on my night stand."

"What note?"

"This one, about some guy named Charlie Harris and his phone number."

"What are you talking about? That's not my handwriting. I don't tilt my letters to the left. You know that," Bill reminded him.

"Well then who left this here? I suppose your intruder left it here by accident."

"Funny, Tom. This makes no sense. Still, maybe we should call the number to see what happens. Maybe he is inside the house like one of those horror movies."

"Let's do it," said Tom as he picked up the phone and dialed. As he completed the number, the paper turned into a fine powder and blew away. "Hey Bill, you see that? I must be still dreaming."

"No, you're not dreaming because I saw it too," Bill said, shaking his head.

As they stood in shock, a voice answered, "This is Beverly Parker. Hello? Hello? Is anyone there?"

"Uh yeah. Is a Charlie Harris there?" Tom managed to say, his voice strained.

"I'm sorry, he's asleep right now. He will be up in a few hours. Are you a friend of his?" Beverly asked.

"Uh...yes. What was your name again, please?" Tom asked.

"My name is Beverly Parker. You sound a little confused. Do you want me to tell him you called?"

"Yeah, that would be good. Let me give you my name and number. My name is Tom Johnson and my number is 555-1354. That's right. Thank you."

Tom hung up the phone. "It was some lady named Beverly Parker. She said Charlie was asleep but would be up in a few hours."

"I know Beverly. She's a nice lady. She's a widow. I did hear that she adopted a child but that was a long time ago." Bill's reminiscing was cut off by the phone ringing.

"Bill Hampton. Can I help you?"

"Sorry to bother you. This is Beverly Parker again. The funniest thing happened. Can I speak to Tom?"

"Sure," Bill said as he passed the phone over to Tom. " Yes maam… We'd love to… Dinner tomorrow night at 7… Got it… Good-bye again."

"What happened?" Bill asked.

"Well, we just got invited to a home cooked meal at the home of Beverly Parker," he replied. "Apparently, this Charlie fellow is there and knew we were going to call."

"I would ask how he knew but I don't want to know. This stuff is too weird for me. I don't understand about that freaky note."

"What is even weirder," said Tom, "Is I used to have a friend in elementary school named Charlie Harris. I wonder if it's the same guy."

As Tom and Bill left to go to Beverly's house, they both felt a little nervous. Bill followed the directions, knowing that area of town well. Finally, they pulled in the driveway of a boxy, aluminum sided, mid-west style ranch.

Bill knocked on the door as Tom glanced away. The door swung opened and there stood Beverly. Her hair was back in a bun and she wore a simple print apron covered in flour. She smiled warmly and welcomed them in. The smell of fried chicken and mashed potatoes filled the air. Bill and Tom started to breathe a sigh of relief.

"Good to see you. Let me get your coats. Dinner is almost done. I'm putting it on the table," Beverly said as she carted their coats away.

"Thank you," they both replied as they looked around. The home was inviting with many cozy decorations and pictures of family. David and Charlie walked into the living room to greet the visitors.

"Hi, I'm Charlie Harris. This is David Parker."

"Good to meet you," Tom replied. "I'm Tom Johnson and this is Bill."

Charlie continued the introductions. "Dave is Beverly's son. Beverly adopted me as a boy. She is definitely the best cook around. I have been with Dave on the mission field in Ethiopia for about three years. We have many things to talk about with you. I know you have many questions, especially about the note. Rest assured, I didn't put it there."

Tom looked incredulous as the realization hit him. "Are you the same Charlie Harris I used to go to elementary school with? And how did you know we were going to call, and the paper?"

Charlie chuckled. "Yes, I am the same Charlie Harris. I think I remember you. And the other question's a long story. I'm going to start with a question. Does the name 'Trojol' mean anything to you?"

Tom hesitated before he recalled the name.

"Uh…Yeah, I remember that name from a dream. Why do you ask?"

"Trojol is a very powerful angel. He is a commander of hundreds of angels, a general of sorts. Even though angels get their assignments from God, they also have supervisors, superiors that they report to and with whom they coordinate their efforts. This may be hard for you to believe, but Trojol has appeared to me twice. The last time, he told me that you would call me here, and that I was to meet with you. He told me many things about you."

Tom hung his head when Charlie said "…many things about you."

Charlie noticed Tom's discomfort and added, "He didn't talk about your past failings; these are forgiven and forgotten. He talked about your future. Things I can't tell you now because you wouldn't believe them. But I will tell you when the time is right. Trojol also said he saved you at a bridge and one of his lieutenants saved a little boy. I think you know what I am talking about," Charlie said.

Tom nodded his head in agreement. He knew there must have been an angel who saved him as he fell hundreds of feet into the river below.

"Dinner's ready," Beverly called. The men gathered around the feast, as the room was flooded with the aroma of the finest of home cooking.

The meal didn't stand a chance against four hungry men caught up in a mystery. The fried chicken was well seasoned and the mashed potatoes had the finest of gravy. They had their fill. Tom turned off his mind as he filled his stomach. It was too much to think about, yet in his heart, he knew this time was coming.

"Tom, you must go with us," said Charlie. "We will travel to Ethiopia after visiting a few churches here in the US to gather support for our journey. It will be the wildest ride of your life but you will grow stronger than you ever thought. The Lord's Kingdom is coming in power."

"Are you asking a question here?" Tom replied as the last bite of apple pie stuck in his throat. He thanked Beverly for the wonderful meal and walked quietly to the living room.

David and Bill looked at Charlie, who was grinning ear to ear. Charlie excused himself and followed Tom into the living room. Tom survey his pursuant and said with a smile, "Its times like these that I wish I could fire up a cigarette."

"Or drink a cold one?" Charlie added, laughing.

"You read me like a book. Did you go to school to learn things like that?"

"Let me show you something," said Charlie. "This is a prayer shawl. It only works through faith in God. It will open your eyes to the spiritual realm if you let it," he said as he draped it across Tom.

Tom sat still and said, "It doesn't work."

"That's because you are not using your faith," Charlie snapped back.

"Ok, fine! Lord open my eyes. I am not afraid of the spirit realm," Tom said as he gazed around the room. After waiting a few minutes and getting additional coaching from Charlie, it suddenly happened.

"Whoa! I see four large angels around each person in the house. Everyone is glowing white. Oh, and there is a black spot in Bill," Tom marveled.

"You have seen enough," said Charlie. "You know that God's power is real. You are to become a vessel of his power and purposes. The Lord has shown me this. He must become greater and you must become less. You know who you were without Him. Now you will find out who you can be with Him."

"Ok, Charlie. You convinced me. Truth be told, I have nothing to lose. I was a messed up piece of junk when God found me. If He wants me, then I'm his. I just hope He knows who he's recruiting," said Tom. Then he added, "By the way, what were those colors I was seeing with the prayer shawl?"

"Black means demonic or death," answered Charlie. "White means they are children of God. The angels are literal and real. You saw our guardian angels. Trojol knows them by name. He will tell you things when you need to know. Don't be afraid to ask. God is pleased with those who seek to know."

"Why is Bill's stomach black and the rest of him is white?" Tom questioned.

"Bill has death in his stomach," Charlie replied.

"It's cancer," said Bill to the stunned room.

"What's all the fussing about?" said David. "Let's pray for the guy. The Lord revealed it to us for a reason."

They prayed and worshipped. Bill went home to get Tom's things while Tom stayed and listened to David and Charlie talk about their adventures.

Tom spent the night at Beverly's house. During the night, He had a dream. He found himself behind the wheel of a car. He heard a voice say, "Go to Rockville Community Church." Before he could react, the car took off, driving itself. He was heading towards an intersection. As Tom entered the intersection, a large truck being driven by a priest or pastor came from the other side. Seeing Tom, he hit the brakes, squealing tires and smelled burning rubber. The truck's trailer started to jackknife. Yet the truck didn't seem to slow down, but accelerated towards Tom's car. There was no time to brace for impact. As the underbelly of the trailer reached his car, Tom woke up.

"I'm ok. I'm ok," he yelled as he arose. His heart pounded with the speed of a hundred horses. He was joined by sympathetic yet curious fellow sleepers who were now very awake.

"What were you dreaming?" asked Charlie. Tom revealed the dream to him. Its meaning was hidden from Tom.

"I know what it means," Charlie replied.

"What?" he asked.

"It means that you and I will be driving separate cars tomorrow, and our first stop is Rockville Community Church."

David and Charlie started laughing.

"That's not very funny," Tom shot back.

"It was funny to me," David chimed in. Tom did not take kindly to the humor.

"See if I tell you my dreams again," Tom fumed.

This made them laugh even more.

As Bill packed up Tom's things, he had a strange feeling that he would not see him again on this side of heaven. Mist came to Bill's eyes as he loaded the last suitcase. It was like losing his son all over again.

Tom approached the door and rang the bell. Bill answered, tears in his eyes. This made Tom feel apprehensive about his trip.

"I don't feel good about you taking this trip. I have a bad feeling about everything," Bill said.

"I'll be fine. I'll be going to Rockville tomorrow. Everything will be great," Tom replied as he tried to hide his own fears about the dream and its meaning.

"Let's pray for your safety," Bill interjected.

"Hey, I'll agree to that," Tom answered.

The prayer didn't ease Bill's mind. They embraced again. "I just feel that this will be the last time we'll see each other on this side of heaven," Bill said.

"Don't be silly," said Tom. "We all prayed for your recovery. Keep the faith. It's just my time to go. I mean…time to go preach and work with Charlie, although I don't really know what I am going to preach. I just know that God set this entire thing up so who am I to resist?"

"You have changed. You're the strong one now and I am the weak one," Bill replied.

"What can I say? You have taught me things that I will never forget. I'll carry the torch," Tom said as the mental image of the tractor-trailer sliding into his car flashed across the eyes of his heart. He remembered the broken glass and twisted metal of his dream. Tom regained his composure but was unable to hide the frightening moment from his friend.

"What did you just see?" Bill demanded.

"Nothing," Tom shot back.

"I know you too well, Tom. I saw the look in your eyes. And why won't David and Charlie ride with you?" Bill probed.

"I've got to go," Tom said as he jumped in the car and took off. This was not the final parting he had planned, but he knew that sharing the dream would yield greater pressure from Bill. There was no way to explain that he was going to be safe, especially since he was not sure of it himself.

After Tom left, Bill started praying for his friend. Soon, Bill was also seeing the images of the crash. He didn't stop his praying until God's peace rested on him. Still, it wasn't enough to calm Bill for his doctor's visit the next day.

Tom sailed down the highway to Rockville, being extremely careful. "I am not going to wreck this time. I am not going to wreck," he said to himself. His forehead and hands were moist. His heart felt like an out of control drummer.

This is crazy. What's wrong with me? Calm down, Tom!

Then it happened. As Tom approached a busy intersection, the traffic lights died. The drivers became confused over right of way. Some gunned it, others stopped. It was total chaos. The driver of an approaching tractor-trailer was sleepy and didn't notice the mayhem until it was too late. He jammed the brakes and jackknifed the truck, just like in Tom's dream. Tom saw it coming and swerved to miss the out-of-control tractor-trailer. As he skidded to a stop without any collisions, Tom breathed a sign of relief. *Whew, that was close*, he thought to himself.

Suddenly, Trojol appeared in the passenger seat and grabbed Tom by the shirt collar. "Get Down!" he shouted, pulling Tom's head down so fast that it slammed into the center console.

A deafening sound of twisting metal blasted right above him. A shower of glass rained down on him. There had not been just one out-of-control tractor-trailer. There had been two. The second one was behind Tom, out of his sight, but nothing was out of Trojol's sight. The angel let go of Tom and disappeared. Tom felt a knot on his forehead as he looked sheepishly out of his newly-formed convertible. Tom felt a strange peace and could only think *Thank God, Thank God,* as he surveyed the wreckage and waited for the police to arrive.

But God wasn't through with this scene yet. Trojol appeared in the cab of the first tractor-trailer. He grabbed the driver and shouted, "You're not supposed to be driving a truck. You are supposed to be a pastor." Before the man had could go into cardiac arrest, the angel disappeared. The man stumbled out of his cab, his knees so wobbly, he could barely walk. A good Samaritan made him sit down until the emergency personnel arrived.

Tom also found himself surrounded by paramedics checking to see if he was OK. Charlie and David arrived just as the paramedics were releasing Tom.

"We heard from the people at church that there was a huge accident at this intersection. We came as fast as we could," they said. "Bill told us that you have a way with accidents. What is it with you and cars?" Charlie's wise crack forced a pained smile from Tom. This time, however, the comic relief was welcomed and appreciated. Tom gave them details of his adventure, especially about Trojol slamming his head down, producing the trophy on his forehead.

"Sounds like you were touched by an angel," Charlie said. They all burst out laughing. "I hope you know you're still going to church this morning. You're not going to get out of it this easy," Charlie continued.

"I kind of thought you would say that," Tom said as he walked gingerly to their car. "Does this blood go with my tie?"

Then Charlie, David and Tom travelled around the country, seeing God work in amazing ways. What they thought would be a few stops, turned in six months of intense ministry. They had one more stop in Philadelphia, PA before they were to fly out of New York City, bound for Ethiopia.

Before they were to speak, David walked into Tom and Charlie's hotel room. "I got an emergency call from the compound in Ethiopia. I have to return right away. Tom, I've applied for your passport and visa to go to Ethiopia. I have some friends in New York City who you can stay with while you wait. It may take some time. You also need to go to the missionary board and get approval. We should have enough documented support to add you on, but they have to look at your application and give the thumbs up. Here are two train tickets to New York and some numbers to call. You will have to hang out until you are cleared to go."

Hang out with Charlie in New York City until the approvals arrived. Two weeks in the Big Apple. That's not too difficult. What could possibly go wrong? Tom thought to himself.

Charlie, however, was having a different reaction. A pale sense of dread began to cloud his thinking. "Why can't I go to Ethiopia and Tom stay in New York until everything is a go?"

"You could, but my contacts with the missionary board are in New York and they are paying all of the expenses. They will need to interview Tom to see if he is fit for duty. He'll also need coaching and encouragement," David replied with a wry smile at Tom.

The discussion over, David left quickly. Later, Charlie drove himself and Tom to the train station, feeling an ache in his heart that started the instant David left them. Tom sensed his friend's sorrow. "Hey, look at it this way," Tom said. "At least I'm not driving."

At a local hospital, Bill was receiving his cancer treatment. As he lay in his bed, another patient was wheeled in to be his temporary roommate. The patient was a young African-American man, surrounded by armed guards. The patient remained still and quiet. Bill, the pastor by nature, struck up a conversation, as he was always in the habit of doing.

"What'cha in for?" Bill inquired.

"Cancer. I don't like hospitals. They creep me out," the stranger replied.

"Yeah, well, I know what you mean. A lot of people die in hospitals. Dangerous places," Bill quipped.

"I hate these wires, these tubes, that nasty smell. What is up with these gowns? Who came up with this stupid crap anyway? I wanna be with *my* people," the stranger replied.

"My name is Bill. What's yours?"

"Slap Dawg. Ain't nobody messin with me. Not none of y'all," he shot back with a look towards his guards now standing at the door.

Undeterred by his façade, Bill asked, "Are you afraid of dying?"

"Naw man! I've looked down the barrel of guns so many times, I can't count. Nothing can stop me. I'm just banged up a little right now."

"What are you banged up about?" he asked.

"Just some crap happened a while back. They call me Slap Dawg cause I put the SLAP on all these cheaters. Ain't nobody pulling one over on me.

This one homey, decides he's going to destroy the goods. I don't know who he thinks he is. Man, I had 50 G's in that stash. He gave me some blow about God and religion. Yeah…whatever man.

Well, he keeps this God crap up. Won't shutup, you know? So I whack him upside the head, blood everywhere. He didn't even fight back. Just some crap about forgiving me. Freaked me out, know what I mean? Dying people's faces never bothered me before, man, but this one had this strange kind of peace like a holy man or something. I'm thinking maybe he did find something and now I done killed my only chance to know what it was.

Then the cops ran up on me one night and I'm in for life. Now, I got this stupid cancer. I guess God's getting' even with me or something."

"Do you know his name?" Bill asked as his lips quivered.

"Yeah, Josh Hampton. I don't know what happened to him. He was my top money maker." Slap Dawg said.

Josh—Bill's son! Tears gushed from Bill's eyes like a river in flood stage. Here was great sorrow and great joy at the same time, realizing that Josh had been saved before he died and that he was safe in the hands of God. Of all of people on earth, only this man could have known. He now knew he would see his son in heaven.

This "chance" meeting sparked many more conversations between Slap Dawg—who later confided that his real name was Clyde Wilcox—and Bill. Bill learned the art of forgiveness and Clyde experienced the Love of God. His life was amazingly transformed. He and Bill formed the most unlikely of friendships.

"Man I ain't ever met no one like you. I'm still tripping cause you can let it slide. Ain't no way I coulda done that. I'd a been all up on somebody for killing my kid," Clyde said.

"Clyde, Christ has forgiven us all for everything. I could never hold anything against you. I just wish I could take you fishing sometime. I think you would like it," Bill said.

"You can't turn me into no redneck. Ain't gonna happen, Bro," Clyde chided.

"You would make a great redneck. You just need some more country music," Bill said as they laughed together.

"Man, thanks for showing me the light. I didn't have nothin to live for, but you done showed me different. I ain't gonna make it much longer. That's what they sayin', anyway. Will you say a little something at my funeral? I want all my peeps to know what life is about. My people need to hear it" Clyde said, holding back the emotion.

"Clyde, I would be honored to speak at your funeral,"

Bill said as the two embraced under the watchful eyes of the guards.

Clyde died a few weeks later. He died with the same peace he saw on Josh's face. Bill spoke at his funeral and was able to comfort Clyde's mom who had stubbornly prayed for her son for 20 years. His words also opened the door for Clyde's friends to hear about the love and forgiveness of Christ.

Chapter 12
New York City

Tom and Charlie were coming to grips with life in New York City. They settled in quickly to the apartment provided by the mission society, and went to the passport processing center to check on the status of their application. Unfortunately, there was no record of their application, so they had to reapply. Despite their best efforts, it was going to take a little longer than they had planned.

One night, the waiting started to take its toll on Tom. "I'm bored. How long is this approval going to take?" he blurted out.

"Well, you didn't do yourself any favors before the missionary board today. Did you really have to comment about their clothes coming from 1960's? Was that totally necessary?" Charlie asked.

"Someone needs to let them know that we are in the twenty-first century," Tom replied.

"I hope you end up in the 60's part of heaven. It would serve you right," Charlie said.

"Well, hey, at least I'll hear some great music," Tom retorted.

There was a knock on the door and Charlie answered. It was a young lady taking up donations for the local Special Olympics event. Tom hollered from behind that they weren't interested. Charlie apologized for his brash friend, gave the lady a donation, and continued talking with her at the door.

Undeterred by the turn of events, Tom continued to verbalize his disapproval of all things "special" when it came to the Olympics. Charlie and his new friend realized they would get no peace within earshot of this obstructionist, so they moved down the hall and talked for 45 minutes. By the time Charlie's bright smile returned to the apartment, his cohort was furious.

"What part of 'no' can't you comprehend?"

"Well for your information," said Charlie with a smile, "I not only gave her our money but I also signed us up as volunteers at the Special Olympics event this Saturday."

"All day? Like 12 hours?" Tom asked.

"Yep. It starts at 8 and ends at 7. I guess that's all day."

"I am not going to spend all day with a bunch of retarded kids," Tom shot back.

Charlie started to reply, but stopped when he noticed someone standing behind his friend. His gaze caused Tom to turn around. Trojol faced Tom and struck him so hard, a large hand print remained on the side of his face.

Charlie winced, then smiled. "I think you have offended our mutual friend. Apparently, he wants us to go." The power from the hit left Tom in excruciating pain. He sank to the floor, his face throbbing. He fell silent as the angel disappeared without a word. He remained on the floor and fell asleep right there.

"Sweet dreams to you, my compassion-challenged friend," intoned Charlie, grateful that the rebuke had not been aimed at him.

Despite the strong non-verbal rebuke, Tom's attitude the next morning had not improved. He continued to think that this type of competition was a big joke or worse: a cruel hoax made up to give the less fortunate the delusions of grandeur. He would soon discover, however, the purpose of his participation as a clear mission to advance the Kingdom of God.

The day of the event started with great pomp and fanfare. The Olympiads strutted around the track, waving to well-wishers in the stands. During this time, Tom began to rub his eyes, feeling strange sensations. A clear whisper broke into his thoughts, "The Angel of Light is here. Tell Charlie." As Charlie was praying, Tom told him about the whisper. They were both confused as to its meaning.

The day continued uneventfully after that, when without warning, Charlie got his one and only assignment for the day. The whisperer said, "The one who wins the girls one-mile run should be congratulated with a big hug."

Mindful of the word he had just received, Charlie watched as the runners rounded the corner. A young female with Down's syndrome led the group. As the crowd cheered her on, Charlie positioned himself to be near the finish line when they crossed. Tom, who did not know Charlie had heard, looked confused.

As Charlie had anticipated, the girl crossed the finish line first. The crowd cheered for the runners as Charlie approached her. She suddenly reached out and wrapped him in a bear hug, squeezing the breath from his ribs. She held him and wouldn't let go. Charlie couldn't get away or even talk. To make matters worse, her father, convinced that Charlie's actions were inappropriate, ran over yelling, "Get your filthy hands off my daughter, you pervert."

The crowd fell silent as they watched the altercation. Tom rushed over to rescue his friend. *Help me!* thought Charlie, but no words could escape his crushed frame. Then the whisperer spoke to Charlie again, "The Angel of Light is here. Release God's power into this child."

Charlie obeyed, managing to mutter words of faith, "I release God's power into this girl."

All at once, a shaft of light appeared 20 yards away, visible only to Charlie. It floated toward them and then the girl saw it too. Charlie grew faint as the shaft of light engulfed them. The girl released Charlie and started to convulse under the power of the light.

The father, not understanding what was happening, lashed out at

Charlie as he rushed to his writhing daughter. "What have you done to my daughter, jerk?"

She continued to groan and shake in the light, then grew calmer. By this time, her mother and teammates had reached the scene. No one could believe their eyes. One of them exclaimed, "Look, God gave Tara a new face."

It was a miracle. Tara's entire DNA's Chromosomal structure had been repaired. She was restored in every way and no longer bore the markings of Down's syndrome. The whole crowd rushed from the stands to see the miracle.

"Charlie, Are you OK?" Tom asked, worried about his friend who was, by now, out cold. "Come on man, wake up," Tom said, shaking him. Charlie woke slowly and sat up, looking around in a daze.

"What happened, Tom? There was the power, and a voice, then everything went black."

Tom described the miracle, and Charlie's mouth dropped open. His heart began praising God, as the joy poured through his mouth. Trojol appeared to Charlie and Tom. "Give glory to God. Take no credit unto yourselves. Come with me now," he said sternly.

They did their best to follow the heavenly messenger, but they had one small interruption when they saw their car blocked by a stretched limousine.

Feeling the need for speed, they jumped into their car, revved the engine and laid on the horn. "Move it, buddy!" Tom shouted out the window in true New York style.

This was enough to cause the owner of the limo to come out from the back. She was a well dressed lady in her forties.

"You boys aren't going anywhere until you answer some questions," she said sternly.

Tom began to argue with her as Charlie began to pray.

Another man, apparently the woman's husband, slipped from the other side of the limo and attempted to introduce themselves. "Sir, I'm sorry for the rude behavior of my wife. It just seemed that you two were leaving before we could thank you for volunteering your time today. Something awesome and holy happened here. We were curious to know who you are. This is my wife Ann, and I am John Wentworth. Ann runs Star Oil Company. I'm afraid she's used to being the boss, even around the house. Please forgive us."

While John was trying to diffuse the situation, Trojol appeared inside the limousine, smirking as he hunkered down in the back seat. He was like a four-year-old playing hide and seek. He caught Charlie's attention, and Charlie whispered the sighting to Tom. It wasn't long before Tom also saw him. John stopped talking when he noticed that Tom and Charlie weren't paying attention to the conversation anymore, but were instead focused on the car. He paused for a second longer and said, "Have you boys ever been in a limousine before?"

To the shock of Ann, who had been fuming on the side while her husband made peace, Charlie said "No, but I would love to." Ann cut off a smart remark when her husband shot her a look that she hadn't seen in a while. She was a tough businesswoman, but knew when to yield. John was a patient man, but he instinctively knew when she had pushed things too far. Which is why she loved him.

Everyone piled in the limo: Tom and Charlie, Ann and John—and Trojol, of course. Ann arranged for someone to return Tom and Charlie's rental car to their apartment.

It took a while for the group to warm up to each other. But since it was a divine appointment, it happened nonetheless. Soon they were sharing their faith in Christ and all that he had done in their lives. They all spent hours sharing their adventures, their dreams, their recoveries, their God. They realized they were part of a club of broken people serving a healing God.

A few days after their meeting, and after much prayer, John and Ann decided to hire Tom and Charlie as full time "consultants" for them. They continued to be missionaries, however, they were now performing different missions.

Chapter 13
The Funeral

Months later, as Tom and Charlie sat in their New York City hotel room, a sense of stagnation seized them.

"Why don't we pray?" Charlie offered.

"I'm tired," Tom replied.

Charlie ignored his friend's response and entered into discourse with their heavenly father. What should have been a prayer of comfort and joy morphed into a long night of spiritual warfare. Charlie remembered from his time in Ethiopia that outward events are just a mask for spiritual reality. After great outward victories, come great spiritual battles. This invisible war never seemed to pick the most convenient time.

"You never know when all hell breaks loose or heaven pours out. We have to be ready my reluctant friend," Charlie said. The verbal jab worked as Tom finally agreed to intercede with him.

They prayed, travailed, wept, and laughed. It was a strange cycle of emotion. Neither understood it, but they allowed the Holy Spirit to intercede through them.

As the night stretched on, the feeling in the pit of their stomach meant no sleep for either of them. Something exciting was draining them. Their strength gave out around 7 am. They both fell asleep, only to be jolted awake a few hours later by the blaring television.

"Why is that thing so loud?" Tom asked. He walked around,

looking for the elusive remote to silence the T.V., while the news anchor proclaimed, "Today we sadly announce the death of Billy Owens, one of the world's best known Christian Evangelists. His ministry spanned over five decades. He had counseled with six presidents and had given four Inaugural Addresses. He was best known for being a uniting figure within Christianity. He will be buried at the Arlington National Cemetery on Tuesday at 4 pm. Three living Presidents and many heads of state will be expected to attend. It will be televised on this station beginning with the honor guard at 3. Now in other news..." Then the television turned off as mysteriously as it had turned on.

"I found the remote. You were sitting on it," Tom said.

"That's a shame," Charlie said.

"It's a shame that I found the remote?"

"No, it's a shame about Billy Owens. I remember meeting him one time. He was quite a preacher," sighed Charlie.

Without warning, a small still voice whispered in Charlie's ear, "Make him preach again." Charlie was stunned. "What's that supposed to mean?" Charlie asked aloud.

"Charlie, who are you talking to?" his roommate inquired.

"I just heard God's voice saying 'Make him preach again'," said Charlie.

An awkward silence settled between the two of them. Finally, Tom looked at his friend with firm resolution and said, "I am not going to DC. Do you hear me, Charlie? No, no, no! Forget it! No way. It ain't gonna happen."

A smile broke out on his Charlie's face. "It's no use. You're going. Start packing your bags."

"Apparently, you and God are completely deaf. I ain't going and that's my final answer."

Charlie looked into Tom's eyes and started laughing.

"What? Is this funny to you?" Tom asked.

"Yes, as a matter of fact it is. The harder you resist, the move convicted you become."

That made Tom smile, despite himself.

"You really think Owens will preach again? You have finally gone off the deep end. You are a certified nut case," Tom said.

"I'm not the one fresh out of rehab," Charlie stated.

"Oh, now that's not fair," said Tom, laughing despite himself.

As they continued to take each other to task, the phone rang and Charlie answered.

"Hotel room 777, can I help you?... Ah, Ann how are you? .... Did I hear about Billy Owens? Yes, I did.... Your corporation has two invitations and you want us to go for you?.... Sure, we would love to go. You can clear it with the authorities. Great! We'll be there. God bless you. Bye." Charlie grinned at Tom.

"No, no, no! What part of no do you not understand?" Tom said.

"It's no use. It's all set. We're leaving," Charlie said as Tom hung his head.

Thirty minutes later, the car sped away with a very reluctant passenger. "If you get tired, I can drive," Tom offered.

Charlie laughed. "No, no, no! What part of 'no crashes' do you not understand?"

"Smart aleck. I hope God embarrasses the crap out of you on Tuesday."

"I believe that's a given," Charlie replied.

Tom soon fell asleep. Having stayed up most of the previous night, Charlie was too tired to keep driving and pulled over to a rest stop. He locked the doors and drifted off to sleep. A few hours later, he was jolted awake by something falling in his lap. It was a warm plate of food. Tom woke at the same time, almost spilling his plate. They both smiled and truly thanked God for their meal. It was no surprise that the meals were their favorites. This assured them even more that they were in God's will, tasked to complete His perfect plan.

Tom and Charlie approached the ornate front desk of the hotel where they would be staying. "Nice place. They don't have hotels like this in Ethiopia," Charlie said.

"There are many things they don't have in Ethiopia," Tom shot back.

"But they have the Power of God. That's something most churches here don't have," Charlie replied.

"One point for you. But you owe me for depriving me of a night's rest," Tom said.

"Hello, Mr. Harris and Mr. Johnson," spoke the desk clerk. "I see that you are preferred guests with Star Oil. We're happy to have you. Here are your keys and an envelope from your CEO. Have a great stay."

The envelope from Ann contained $2000, event passes, and a note. "Buy a nice suit and try to stay out of trouble. These tickets are Star Oil seats. Remember that you are representing the corporation."

Charlie was glad to see the money but the note put a lump in his throat. Tom read it and laughed. They purchased their suits and finally got a good night's rest, figuring it might be a while until they got another one.

In the morning, Tom and Charlie walked through the lobby and past a group of children. Tom noticed that each child was staring at them.

"Charlie, those kids are all watching us. Have they never seen a white man and a black man together before?" Tom asked.

"It's probably spiritual. Things like this happened a lot in Ethiopia. Demeke told me that young children often see angels around people. It causes them to stare at you," Charlie replied.

"How many angels are around us?" Tom inquired.

"Enough to match the coming warfare. I'm not sure I'm feeling comfortable right now," Charlie confided.

"Me neither," Tom added.

They found a shuttle and arrived early. They passed security and picked up a program of the burial service. Reverend R.J. Drakes was scheduled to speak. Charlie remembered him from Sunday morning TV—a large African-American man from the South with fiery passion for preaching the gospel. Charlie grinned, imagining Drakes' style in this venue.

As they read their programs, a member of the secret service asked them to come with him. He walked them all the way to the VIP section on the second row. "Here are your seats," the agent said before disappearing into the crowd. Charlie pointed out to Tom that R.J. Drakes was walking up the aisle.

"This is so cool. I've never been this close to the big wigs," Charlie whispered as Tom smiled. Then R.J. Drakes walked up to Charlie and started talking to him.

"Charlie Harris, can you be my assistant today? I just need you to come up on the stage with me. There will be a chair for you. If I need something, I'll just motion to you for help. Do you think you can do that?" Drakes asked.

Charlie gulped in the affirmative, and Drakes smiled as he walked away. Unbeknownst to Charlie, Trojol had also visited with Drakes and gave him those instructions. Charlie and Tom stared at each other with astonishment.

"Is this happening?" Charlie asked.

"I don't know. Pinch me to see if I am awake," Tom answered.

As the day progressed, they saw the Who's Who of the rich and famous stride into the funeral. Four different presidents, wealthy businessmen, and foreign dignitaries from all over the world took their seats. Tom and Charlie sat among them. The secret service were everywhere, talking to each other on small, concealed headsets. It was a beehive of activity and excitement. Tom was enjoying himself, but Charlie started sweating and rubbing his hands.

"Why are you so nervous?" Tom asked.

"I don't know. I have this bad feeling that God is going to ask me to do something I can't do," Charlie whispered.

"I think that's the norm with Him. You know what it says about 'fear not.' That's what those angels are always saying just before they ask you to do something impossible," Tom reassured his friend with a mock grin.

"I need to get out of here," stammered Charlie.

"What, and leave these awesome seats. You have got to be kidding," Tom retorted.

Charlie tried to get up to leave and noticed that his suit coat was stuck in the chair. "No, no, no, this can't be happening. Tom, help me get this thing loose."

"I'm not helping you. I think you're supposed to stay right there," Tom replied. "Beside, just what part of 'no'…"

Tom's jest was cut off by Charlie's glare.

The music started to play while Charlie tried once more to free his coat without anyone noticing. Then he heard it tear. "Oh great, now I will look like a total idiot in front of everyone," Charlie whispered.

"You mean there was a time when you weren't a total idiot?" Tom asked, still teasing.

"You're not helping right now," Charlie shot back, wishing he could laugh just to relieve the tension. Instead, he sat back down and concluded it was no use trying to leave. God was going to do what he was going to do.

As the service progressed, various dignitaries spoke of Billy's life and work, from his preaching crusades to helping widows and orphans. Throughout the speeches, Charlie noticed one of the secret service men staring at him. It made him feel uncomfortable. *Geeze, are these guys profiling me?* he wondered. *Ah, come on, get over it. They're watching everybody the same way.*

Yet the agent continued to stare throughout the service. Even the socially obtuse Tom noticed it. In a lighthearted attempt to ease the tension, Tom initiated a "no-blink" contest with the agent, but soon gave up.

"Charlie, that guy hasn't blinked in like…5 minutes. That can't be natural. And did you see his eyes? They are brilliant blue, like they are on batteries or something," Tom whispered.

Charlie, meanwhile, was in the midst of a personal struggle while the staring contest was being contested. *No God, I can't do this. Whatever it is, I can't, not now, not here.*

Finally, the keynote speaker—R. J. Drakes—took the stage. Like a man on the road to perdition, Charlie arose and followed Drakes, taking his misgivings, torn suit, and faith in Almighty God with him.

"Go get'em slugger," Tom whispered, not realizing the prophetic nature of his words. Charlie took a seat on the stage behind Drakes.

Drakes started his sermon. "Today before you lies a man. This man gave his life for the gospel. He was blessed in every way, but most of all, he was a blessing to all those he touched."

Drakes continued his sermon in his immutable style. The crowd was enthralled.

"Let me speak briefly about the gospel he preached. In 1 Corinthians 1, starting in verse 17, 'For Christ did not send me to baptize but to preach the gospel – not with words of human wisdom, lest the cross of Christ be emptied of its power. For the message of the cross is foolishness to those who are perishing, but to us who are being saved, it is the power of God.' My friends, Billy Owens did in fact preach the gospel. He preached the cross of Christ. He preached it in Africa. He poured himself out there. He spoke of the cross that saves us. The cross that contains the ultimate power of a changed life. No one who heard him remained untouched by his sincerity, his integrity, his passion for God."

While the audience was mesmerized by Drakes preaching, Charlie was jarred from his reverie when the secret service agent who had been staring at him, touched his shoulder.

"Sir, I believe this is yours."

It was a Hillerich and Bradsby Louisville Slugger baseball bat. Not realizing what was transpiring, Charlie looked it over. It was identical to the one he had as a child. He remembered how it helped save his life. He stopped his study of the blunt instrument when it sunk in that this was not just a replica—it was the very bat taken from his home hundreds of miles away. The secret service member continued his glare of Charlie, revealing brilliant blue eyes. As Charlie gripped the bat and locked onto those heavenly eyes, he could hear a whisper that made him shudder.

"I want you to take the bat and hit the coffin when I tell you to," the whisperer said.

That's when all of Charlie's strength left him. He turned away from the agent and stared at the stage floor. *I can't do that*, he thought, knowing that God would hear his thoughts.

"I didn't ask for your approval, only your obedience," the whisperer returned.

A dozen reasons to not obey filled his head. *I'll be arrested. I'll be humiliated. I'll be…, I'll be… I'll be obedient.*

Drakes sermon continued.

"Let me tell about when Christ came into my life. I was a lost teenager, groping in the darkness. My heart was looking for the light. Little did I know that it resided between these pages," said Drakes as he held up a worn Bible.

The whisperer spoke again to Charlie, "Now! Hit the coffin with everything you have."

Tears of anguish tore down Charlie's face. He knew it was time. He felt like the last sane man on earth about to jump off a cliff.

Charlie stood and no one seemed to notice. As he walked slowly to the casket, Drakes shared his salvation experience .

"And when Christ dropped into my life…"

A thunderous crack echoed from the hollow wooden casket, followed by the clink of the casket's metal handle striking the floor.

"Yes, that's what it sounded like when Christ landed in my heart," Drakes said, not missing a beat as if he knew the precise moment the bat would strike.

The whisperer spoke another time. "Hit it again and again until the casket is destroyed."

Charlie figured he had nothing to lose at this point, so he tore into the coffin with all his might and then some. The oak box soon fell apart from the repeated blows. The auditorium doors closed without human hands and locked automatically. No one was getting in or out. Some panicked, thinking it was a terrorist plot. Pandemonium broke out. The secret service members seemed to be part of the conspiracy, as they stood motionless. The television anchors were filming and giving their commentary. The DBC network was reporting a race riot had broken out during the funeral and that two black men had stormed the stage to vent their anger at white America. The other networks were confused but were letting the tape roll.

John Wentworth caught a glimpse of the "Race Riot" on T.V. and called for Ann. "Honey, come quickly. You have got to see this. It's your boys causing a ruckus in DC."

"What?!" She responded as she ran to the television set. "Oh my, what are they doing?" she gasped. She picked up her cell phone to call Tom. She figured Charlie was too "busy".

Tom felt the vibration and saw the call was coming from Ann. "Ann," he replied in a whisper. "What's up?"

The response was filled with fury. "What do you mean 'What's up?' I am going to kill you two. What are you doing? Starting a bar room brawl?" she yelled.

"Sorry, gotta go. The show's still on," he said as hung up the phone. *She sounded mad. I wonder why?* he thought as he grinned.

The whisperer continued speaking to Charlie with finality, "Now, pull the body out of the casket, command life into it, throw it down, and you'll be done for now."

Charlie pulled the lifeless corpse from the tattered casket. The whole congregation gasped. Charlie screamed with all the faith he could muster, "I command life into this body." He hurled the dead man unceremoniously across the stage. Billy Owens' body flopped down in an awkward angle. His ashen white form laid in a heap. Unperturbed, Drakes continued his sermon. "The Bible says that one day the final enemy will be defeated. The last enemy to be destroyed is death. For He has put everything under his feet. Christ has defeated death once and for all on the Cross."

Then Drakes quoted I Corinthians 15:54-55, "When the perishable has been clothed with the imperishable, and mortal with immorality, then the saying that is written will come true: Death has been swallowed up in victory. Where…,"

Suddenly, the presence of God filled the stage. Reverend Drakes could not continue. He just started to weep, falling to his knees, as did Charlie and everyone else near the stage.

Drakes tried to finish the 55th verse again. "Where …." He started weeping again. A wave of glory came in a cloud descending onto the stage. Drakes tried once more, "Where…," but he was interrupted for the last time.

"Where, O death is your victory? Where, O death is your sting?" The voice came from a man standing beside Drakes. It was Billy Owens. He was alive and well, and barefooted.

"Pardon my lack of footwear. I seemed to have misplaced my shoes,"

Then Billy grinned broadly and began his sermon, taking over where R.J. Drakes had left off. Every eye was on Billy. In cafes, restaurants, and living rooms all across the world, people watched as the once-dead evangelist, known and loved throughout the world, was about to preach a sermon that would impact the world.

The secret service team members grabbed Tom and Charlie, and quickly escorted them out for their protection. "Be careful to not take any credit for what happened here," the agent-angels told them. A feeble "OK" was all they could offer up as they gratefully disappeared from the chaotic scene.

News reports of the event varied. Some networks chose not to even air it. The DBC network actually retracted their original story of a race riot and reported the miracle in its entirety. The public reaction was mixed. Many were deeply impacted and chose to follow Christ, seeing His power to resurrect. Others scoffed and said it was all a put-on.

Afterward, many people from all over the world came to see R.J. Drakes and Billy Owens preach. Their ministries exploded. Oddly enough, no one seemed to know the name of the two young men who facilitated it all. They managed to escape notoriety and lived to tell of it.

Chapter 14
Ali Hassan

Ali grew up a Muslim in war-weary Afghanistan. He pursued his learning with great vigor, and his quest for understanding was insatiable. He memorized large portions of the Koran as a child, amazing his friends and family. The mosque meetings were the highlight of his dull existence.

Dark-skinned with tightly napped black hair, he looked like everyone else his age, but his family recognized his potential early. They taught him to read and sacrificed much for his education. His goal in life was to be an Imam at the local mosque.

When Ali was 14, his world changed forever. His village had staged a revolt against the occupying Soviets. In retaliation, his entire village, including his family: father, mother, brothers and a sister, were killed while he was away. His outlook on life became a seething mix of chaos, paranoia and rage, devouring what used to be a bright and eager mind. As he surveyed the crater that was once his peaceful home, he vowed destruction to the infidels—to all infidels. He determined to strike back any way he could. His happy life was gone forever, replaced by a new and grim reality.

Yet questions remained. During prayer, Ali would silently ask, *Why is there all this chaos? Why is there so much evil in the world?*

The Imams told him that everything was the will of Allah. He struggled with this concept. It seemed too fatalistic, as if no one made choices of their own. God's will appeared dark and mysterious.

Then Ali heard of a shadow army that was resisting his country's occupiers. Having no way of carving out anything but a starvation existence on his own, he sought out the secretive group and eventually was accepted by them.

Ali found a new hope and self-respect through this group of mujahedeen–holy warriors of sorts. The leadership was internationally based, aligned with Al-Qaida. Ali was hungry for a different life, one in which he could fight back and make a difference–no longer a victim. He desired to be a hero like the ancient warriors. He trained well and moved up quickly in the ranks. His superiors found he could be trusted. He felt a deep acceptance among the brotherhood.

True to his nature, however, Ali began to entertain questions. He once dared to offer his concerns outwardly, and quickly discovered the harsh penalty for individual thought. Still, it was a small price to pay for the identity he desperately needed. He wisely learned to keep some ideas and questions to himself.

Yet a yearning spirit cannot be buried, and many years after joining, he began to feel like an outsider. Everything felt awkward. He couldn't explain it. At times, he wanted to get out of the organization. He was growing in a different direction and did not understand it.

During this time, Ali started having vivid dreams. They would strike at unusual times. He saw things he didn't want to see. He saw the explosions and deaths before they happened. He saw who would desert first. Ali shared his dreams with a few trusted brothers. Some saw the dreams as a gift. Others saw them as evil or a sign of weakness. It seemed to divide the group.

High level leadership discussed the dilemma of Ali at length. A month later, a decision was made. Ali waited tensely for the final word. His judgment was an assignment in Jordan. Ali was to be establish in a sleeper cell—a link that would allow him to blend in for now, and eventually buy weapons and smuggle them back to Afghanistan.

He would study Arabic and English at the university level in preparation.

Part of Ali's assignment was to find permanent work in Jordan and use it as a cover. It would take time to find an arms dealer who would sell with no questions asked.

Ali did not like the assignment but was eager to show his faithfulness to the cause. He also wanted to be away from so many prying eyes. He had never been to Jordan. He had no clue what would transpire there. Yet God knew where he was going. He had sent his messenger ahead of Ali.

All the while, the dreams continued and increased in their intensity. Waking up in the middle of the night, sweating and panting, became Ali's normal routine. These episodes left him shaken and afraid—two emotions he did not care for. Still, Ali grew curious about the dreams' meaning, and he hoped that the meaning would be the cure. He wanted the dreams to stop, but he also wanted to understand the hidden world from where they came.

As Ali left the compound after his judgment, he had a strange feeling that he would return one day. His friends wished him well. "Allah is great," and "Allah's will be done," was echoed in their farewells. Despite the well-wishes, Ali felt lonely, empty, and scared. *Shouldn't I feel joyful, triumphant, fulfilled, or least happy?* In his innermost heart, he felt he was doing something wrong, something to be ashamed of. *These feelings are my weakness. Allah's will prevails*, he told himself.

Silence filled the SUV as Ali and a few select brothers trekked across the desert for two days. Ali was given enough money to fly to Amman, Jordan and live for 2 weeks. He would have to find work fast. *Allah's will be done,* he repeated to himself.

The next night, Ali had a dream in which he saw himself returning to his friends hiding in the mountains. He said to them, "Brothers, look what I have found." He opened his hands, revealing a brilliant light. Some of his friends became enthralled with the colorful beauty; others became angry. A fierce disagreement emerged among them.

Then Ali saw a coffin being lowered into the dirt with an inscription, "Ali Hassan, Hero of Islam." He watched as the dirt was piled on his chest, feeling a huge weight that kept him from breathing.

Ali awoke from the dream, panting and afraid. It took a few minutes to realize he was still on the plane to Amman.

After this dream, Ali doubted if he was strong enough to fulfill his mission. Was he going to die? Fear gripped him as he tried to erase the dream's images from his mind. He needed help and spiritual counsel. He decided to look for a mosque and share these experiences with an Imam. He hoped this would bring him the solace he needed to continue as a soldier of Islam. This hope filled Ali with peace again. *God will help me. They will see. I am not weak. I will show them. I am stronger than they think.* He feel back asleep and slipped into a dream so powerful, it would eclipse all the other dreams for its impact on his life.

Ali knelt in the mosque at prayer time. His life had changed drastically in the two years before coming to Jordan. His understanding was growing clouded but his desire to do the will of Allah was stronger than ever. As he prayed and closed his eyes, scenes from his dream flashed through his mind. He had to open his eyes quickly before the scenes gripped him and challenged his faith. He couldn't understand their meaning. The images were so real. Ali believed that Allah gave dreams, but this contradicted everything he knew, everything that was familiar to him.

As he finished his prayers, a man approached him saying, "The Imam will see you now."

"Thank you," Ali replied, rising to his feet. Ali stayed very quiet as he walked to the secret room. This needed to be a private conservation. Ali could not let the others know that his faith was wavering. *Maybe the Imam can help me.*

Ali's escort opened the door and the Imam greeted Ali from inside the room. "Ali, come in and sit down. It is so good to see you. You have grown so strong in your faith."

Ali remained quiet. He didn't know how to begin. Ali was usually a man with no fear. He was always called the "Brave One" in battle. But this day, he was scared and confused. After an awkward silence, the Imam said, "You must be troubled. Tell me what has caused this trouble."

"I had this dream," began Ali tremulously. "I know it is blasphemous but I cannot understand its meaning. I don't understand why I had it. I have served without fear for many years, yet fear clings to me now. Maybe Allah has found something unclean in me and has decided to punish me for my weaknesses."

"Well, tell me the dream and we shall see," the Imam replied.

"It was very misty," began Ali. "I was in a dark robe. I had a machine gun. It was very powerful. When men attacked me, I could destroy them. The gun was so strong that my enemies would split into pieces. I saw no defeat before me. Suddenly my heart started to hurt and blood started pouring from my chest even though I was not wounded. My gun slipped from my hands as a man in a white robe approached me. I reached and picked it up. The man had gone back into the mist. I kept trying to find him."

Ali continued, "When I saw him again, he was caring for a child who was wounded. As I looked, I saw that the child was me as a boy. The man looked at me with the most beautiful eyes, beyond any eyes I have ever seen. It was as though he could see right through me–like he was looking into my soul. He started to speak and lightning shot through me but it did not injure me. I sank to my knees; I was crying out for mercy. What he said I will never forget.

He said, 'Ali, I love you and I have called you. You are to be mine. Seek me and you will find me.'

I asked, 'Who are you?'

He said nothing but I could hear someone in a distance whisper the name "Isa." I started weeping as a strange presence covered me. He reached inside my chest and I could feel him grabbing my beating heart. He said, 'Ali, I am healing your heart.' As I kneeled, the fog lifted, revealing that I was on top of a large hill. There were millions of people bowing to this man. They were worshipping him. Then the dream ended," Ali said.

"I do not understand why you feel that this is blasphemous. It sounds like Isa is calling you," The Imam said.

Ali was shocked. He couldn't believe what he was hearing.

"You do not think that I am condemned for such a dream?" said Ali, trembling. "How can I seek this man? I do not know who he is. I once heard that dreams like this are evil. But there is more. When I awoke from the dream, I saw this on my chest."

Ali opened his shirt to reveal a human size hand print on the left side of his chest. It was right over where his heart would be. It was a brand, a permanent mark that could never be removed.

The Imam remained silent. This spoke volumes to Ali. Then the Imam said something that shook Ali to his core, "I have had a similar dream." He also opened his shirt to reveal the same type of hand print over his heart. "Isa also appeared to me. I have searched and found Him. I have received His forgiveness and healing. He has become my Savior. But you must not speak of our talk with anyone. I would be killed for such a statement. You are not the first one in this mosque who has had these dreams. I have prayed that others would understand and seek the forgiveness of Isa. You are one of many that I have prayed for. It is no accident that you are here speaking with me about this. These things are what I pray for. I cannot tell you everything. You must seek for yourself. I will pray that you will understand about Him soon."

If Ali was speechless before the meeting, he was seven times more speechless afterwards. Despite the confusion, however, he felt a warmth in his chest. He sensed that it was God's will for this meeting to happen. It was the first time something so supernatural had happened to him. Ali decided he would continue his journey for understanding.

Later that night, as Ali slept, he had another dream. He was in his small apartment in the middle of Amman. He heard the voice of a small girl calling out in Arabic, "He is here. Can't you see Him? He is right here. This is wonderful. He is here." Ali went around the apartment trying to find the door to get out. In his desperation, he grew afraid. Then he discovered a hall ending with a door and a cross on it. Ali touched the cross and the door opened by itself. He stepped outside to find a crowded marketplace. Still, he continued to hear the girl's voice. He walked in the general direction of the sound, rounded a corner and found a girl shouting, "He is here."

Ali ran to her and asked, "Where is this person?"

She replied, "He's right behind you. He has been chasing after you for your entire life."

Ali froze in his tracks and slowly turned around. There was the man again. Ali reached out to touch Him. Ali felt a surge of warmth and peace that he had never known. His heart started racing wildly.

The man said, "Finally, you have turned to me."

Then Ali woke up.

Ali rose up from the bed with the images from the dream still burning in his mind. He felt a peace he couldn't understand. He went to work that day and couldn't shake the peace. It permeated his whole being. Yet it made no sense. After work, he took a different way home and saw someone making a painting. When he stopped to look, he saw that it was the same young girl. As Ali stared at her, she looked at him and spoke, "I know why you are here."

Ali was stunned. Two things took him by surprise. One was that the girl knew him. The other was that she had the same voice as in the dream.

"You do?" he stammered.

"Yes," she said. "Can you wait here a moment while I bring you something?" she asked.

"OK," he replied.

She went in her house and quickly emerged with a beautiful

painting. It was a portrait of Jesus. "When I close my eyes, I see Him. He brings me peace. He will bring you peace too," the girl said.

The sight of the picture took Ali's breath away.

"He is called Isa by some," continued the girl, "and he is called Jesus by others. He is the one you are seeking. He has pursued you all of your life. He is calling you even now. You need only to let him into your heart. Here is my Bible. You can learn about Him."

Ali stood with tears running down his face as joy flooded his heart. He had no words to say. It was a divine moment. He had been touched by the Almighty.

After gaining his composure, he told the girl, "Thank you. You are truly an angel of God."

"You're welcome," she replied simply.

"I'm crying and I don't know why. I don't understand this," Ali said.

"You are realizing how good God is to you. You are sensing His kindness. He is pursuing you with His love. Your heart just can't resist Him anymore," the girl said.

"He is good to me. I am starting to see," Ali replied. "Thank you so much. What is your name?"

"I'm Abida," she said. "God Bless you."

Ali left with the picture and the Bible carefully stowed under his clothes. He had never seen a Bible before, but knew that others would not understand.

As the months passed, Ali devoured the Bible, reading it day and night. Everything started to make sense to him. He spent many hours reading about Jesus. He knew God had led him to this point. For the first time in his life, Ali started living with the peace of God. It consumed him, but he had a problem. *Who can I talk to about what has happened to me?*

He started to have thoughts that didn't seem to be his own. It was like God was talking to him in his thoughts. The thoughts kept saying to find others who knew about Jesus.

In obedience to these feelings, Ali began to ask around the

neighborhood. He was very careful not to ask the wrong people. He soon found a church with people who welcomed him. He made friends quickly. The people in the church were amazed to hear about the story of his journey. Ali found he wasn't alone. Others had had equally powerful encounters with the risen Christ. Some of them also shared their stories of dreams, visions, and miracles on their path of discovery.

Ali grew in many ways; however, there was a deep secret he had hidden from everyone. He was part of an Al Qaeda cell, based in Afghanistan. He knew that one day, the group would catch up to him. If they knew about his conversion, he would most likely be killed. After months of prayer, he approached his pastor.

"I need to talk to you about something," Ali told him.

"Ali, what is it my brother. You look worried."

"Can we meet somewhere privately?" Ali requested.

"Sure."

They met later that day in the pastor's study. Ali blurted out his secret. "Pastor, before I knew Jesus, I was an ardent follower of Islam. I was very zealous for Jihad. I trained in Afghanistan for Al Qaeda. I was with them for many years and I pledged my life to the cause. They sent me to Jordan to await orders. They have not contacted me in a while but I feel the time will be soon that they will call on me. If I refuse them, they will kill me. Pastor, I cannot now do what I vowed to do back then. Jesus has made me into a different person. If they knew that I follow Christ, they would hunt me down. I wish I could speak to them about Christ. Maybe they would turn to Him like I did. But more likely, they would kill me ."

"Ali, have you seen anyone from this group?" the pastor asked.

"I have seen no one. But my heart tells me it will be soon."

"Well, let's pray that you will have wisdom. The Bible promises that if we ask for wisdom we will receive it," the pastor offered.

"Yes, let's pray. May His will be done," Ali replied.

The pastor started to pray.

"God, we come to you. We pray that you would give Ali wisdom to know what to do. I pray for his protection. I pray for the angels to surround him and keep him safe. I pray that no harm will come to him. He will be guided by your Holy Spirit."

As the prayers continued, Ali's eyes misted. The pastor knew something was touching him in the Spirit.

"Ali, why are you crying?"

"I believe I know what to do. I am supposed to go to them," Ali said.

"You can't be serious. I don't think I could stand to see you do that. That's too dangerous."

"I know it sounds crazy, but I feel it's what I must do."

"Well, let's pray that God would confirm this if it is what He wants," the pastor offered, and Ali agreed. They prayed, cried, and hugged each other as Ali left.

That night, Ali had another dream. He was in his room packing his suitcase for a long trip. He was looking for something when he opened the closet door. There was an angelic host standing there.

The angel held out a piece of armor and said, "You almost forgot this. The Lord says *I will send my angel to be with you for you are going into the lion's den. They cannot harm you for I have ordained you to go to them. You shall not fear them because they cannot touch you. You are mine and I have put my shield around you.*"

Ali woke up from the dream. Although it was three in the morning, Ali called his pastor. To Ali's surprise, his pastor was already awake. "Pastor, I believe I have the confirmation. I had a dream. It was very clear."

"I know. I had a dream too. God bless you, my brother. I'll never stop praying for you," his pastor replied as his voice started to crack.

"God bless you, pastor. You've been a light for me," Ali said as he hung up the phone. Tomorrow was going to be the start of a long journey.

That same night at a hotel in Atlanta, Tom also had a dream. He saw a hungry and battered child speaking a foreign language. The child kept repeating the same phrase. Tom knew the child was hungry but he didn't have anything to feed him. Moments later, the child was in Tom's arms. A hand reached around him and touched the child. Tom turned around to see where the hand had come from. He saw a blinding light.

Tom woke up to a pitch black room. He fell out of bed trying to reach the light switch. He was so disoriented that he ran into a wall and hit the floor again. Stunned but determined, he found the switch and turned it on. Charlie was awake and sitting on the couch, still up. They looked at each other and knew what the other was thinking.

Tom blurted out, "I'm going back to bed. I'll pack tomorrow. You call Ann and get us tickets."

Charlie laughed and said, "Afghanistan is nice this time of year."

Tom shook his head and said, "I hope there is an in-flight movie."

Charlie closed his eyes and chuckled. He laid down to go to sleep, finally feeling like the reason for his insomnia was fulfilled. He was going to need his rest; it was going to be a long flight.

Unknown to Charlie and Tom, God had already worked out a plan involving an engineer who Ann's company had fired five years previously. The day before Tom's dream, Ann found out the engineer was in Kandahar, Afghanistan, working for a Christian relief organization. She wanted to offer him his old job again. He had been fired for sharing Christ with some children in Kuwait. The company, at the time, was sensitive to local unrest. Firing the engineer seemed the only prudent course.

When Charlie called, Ann cut him off before he could explain anything, saying, "Charlie, I need you to go to Kandahar, Afghanistan. Find Ed Waxman. He's a former employee of Star Oil and I want to hire him again. I'll wire you the money for the tickets, set up a hotel room, and a rental car. I hope they still rent cars there. Where are you guys, anyway?"

"We're in Atlanta at the Service Inn on Dunnberry Street. We'll find our passports," Charlie said as he hung up the phone, shaking his head.

"That was quick," said Tom. "What's up?"

"It's all done. God's already worked it all out. Just find your passport and we'll be on our way."

Tom was starting to get used to the notion that a life of faith was always going to be like this. He was living the dream, and laughed inwardly at his own unintended pun. Tom never stopped being amazed at the awesomeness of God.

This trip would be the final leg of Tom and Charlie's journey together. They both sensed it. Charlie knew they were going to soon part ways and Tom would soon be on his own. That was OK with Charlie, as long as they remained united in Christ.

The flight to Afghanistan was filled with an eerie silence, interrupted only by Charlie's hushed prayers. Tom also quietly prayed. He felt so strange that he skipped the in-flight movie—his favorite part of any flight—to listen for God's whispers in his heart.

Two flights and several time zones later, they finally landed in Kabul, where a message was waiting for them. Ann left instructions for the car, hotel, and the location of the relief center where Ed Waxman was working. From her detailed instructions, they quickly located Ed.

As Tom tried to introduce himself and Charlie, Ed turned and handed him a starving boy. Through unkempt hair and tattered clothes, all hope seemed to be drained from the boy's eyes. The boy was six years old and had not eaten a meal in 34 days. When the volunteers found him, he was just skin and bones. They tried to feed him but to no avail. The only thing that seemed to help was to spoon feed him some milk.

As Tom held the boy, the boy's eyes lit up. Then the boy reached up and hugged him. It surprised Tom that the lifeless figure responded to him like that. The dying boy said "thank you" in his Pashtun language, then closed his eyes and passed away in Tom's arms.

Tom was not emotionally prepared for this, and quickly handed the corpse back to Ed. Frantic for some tangible means of contributing, Tom and Charlie spent the rest of that day digging the boy's grave and searching for any relatives.

After a long search, they found the boy's sister at the center. They brought Ed to be an interpreter and talk to the little girl. As they explained how her brother died, she bowed her head and cried. When she could speak, she told Ed how they had arrived at the center. Her parents had died in the war. She and her brother were without food for a very long time. Her brother had a dream that the Prophet Isa would take them both to heaven, but only after they met a white-skinned foreigner who would show love to them. She said that she now knows her brother is in heaven. Then she asked Tom and Charlie to teach her everything they knew about Isa, to which they joyously agreed.

She said, "My brother never stopped believing that he would find you. We walked 47 miles to Kandahar because he said there was a city in his dream and Kandahar was the only city that he knew of."

Tom didn't know how to respond. "I wished I had of been here earlier. Maybe I could have saved your brother from starving."

"You are here to do God's business," the girl said through the interpreter. "He brought you here when He meant to. My brother is in heaven and I am a believer because of you."

———◦((◉))◦———

True to his convictions, Ali saved enough money and flew back to Afghanistan. He was nervous and tried not to think of the price his convictions might carry. Yet his confidence in the Lord had never been stronger. He spent his time on the plane singing some of the songs he had learned at church.

This is going to be a long flight, he thought to himself as he pulled out his Bible and started reading Psalms 91. "No harm shall befall you and no disaster will come near your tent. He will command His angels to lift you up."

Ali thought about the angels being around him. Peace covered him like a warm blanket on a cold night. He had never felt peace until he met Jesus. He recalled the dream where he saw Him; those brilliant blue eyes cut right through him, exposing his need and healing his blindness.

When Ali finally left the plane, he had no plan, only a purpose. He stayed in the airport and prayed. After three hours, he felt he should go into town. He started walking and praying. He was hesitant to look anyone in the eye for fear he would be recognized. *I must be crazy. Why am I doing this?* He continued walking and humming for about 8 miles. It was so hot, his lips were parched. He dropped into a small roadside stand for a quick drink. The stares left him uncomfortable.

"What are you here for?" a stranger asked.

"I'm delivering relief supplies," he said without rehearsal.

"Good, they are needed," the stranger replied, noting Ali's accent as local.

As he left the store, a woman looked him in the eye and said, "Get ready. Things will happen fast." Then she disappeared as quickly as she had emerged. No one else seemed to notice her.

What things are to happen fast? What is she talking about?

Ali's immediate need was to figure out where to stay for the night. He remembered there were a few rooms where he could stay in town. It would be just a few miles up the road. He continued walking and found the place. It was very busy.

"We have no rooms here. Too many relief workers. Come back tomorrow," the man at the front responded.

"What do I do now?" he asked, to no avail.

Ali started to cross the bridge in the middle of town and couldn't believe his eyes. He saw an old comrade in arms from years before.

"Rasheed, is that you?" he blurted out. The man pretended not to notice.

Ali continued his persistence, "Rasheed, is that you? It has to be you. I remember the scar on your chin." Ali started to follow him. The man quickened his pace, but Ali was not going to lose him. They had known each other too well.

Ali caught up with him as Rasheed turned around and said loudly, "No Ali, don't come any closer." He partially opened his clothes revealing his bomb vest.

When this happened, chaos erupted. Women ran to their children. People scattered like sheep as screams filled the air. While everyone else panicked, Ali and Rasheed stood still and looked at each other. They had been such close friends until their lives took very different paths. Rasheed had become more militant and desperate while Ali had discovered God's love and peace. They started a final and desperate dialogue.

"Ali, don't come closer. I must do this for Allah," He stated with deep sadness.

"No Rasheed, this is not what God wants you to do," Ali spoke with a deep love for his friend.

"I am willing to serve Allah and His prophet in whatever he says," he said.

"Rasheed, I have found God. He is not like that. He is loving. He will heal our people. This jihad will do nothing but bring more misery, more death." Ali spoke with an authority he had never experienced before.

"Ali, it's too late for me," Rasheed said.

Ali ran to his friend. As they collided, they both fell from the bridge into the river. They were not alone in their fall. Ali could clearly see and feel the angel embrace him moments before the blast went off.

The impact of the explosion was greatly diminished under the water, yet it still carried a lethal punch. The shrapnel shot though the water but no particles struck Ali, even though he was only a few feet away from the bomb's epicenter. However, the shock knocked Ali unconscious. Trojol was able to transport him to the shore to prevent him from drowning. The searchers found Ali battered and bruised, but still alive on the river bank.

When he awoke, he was surrounded by Afghani police and American Soldiers. They roused him and sent him to the hospital under heavy guard. While in transport, they rifled through his personal items. They noticed that he had just arrived from Jordan complete with passport and plane ticket. They started asking questions and never stopped.

Meanwhile, the police were speaking with the townspeople to determine what happened. The witnesses were giving conflicting information. Some people claimed seeing two men fall into the river while some claimed that three men fell in. The American soldiers combed the river for more bodies but only found some of Rasheed's clothes and his bomb belt. They continued to seek the mysterious third man. Ali refused to tell them anything. Some witnesses said that Ali pushed the bomber into the river. Ali was not charged, although he was held for a long time for interrogation.

The next day, a nurse came in to help Ali with his bandages. The guard left the room to give him his privacy, and stood outside. The nurse spoke quietly to Ali in Pashtun. "Your friend Rasheed is alive. He said an angel protected him. He knows he should have died but doesn't understand why he was spared. He did lose his left arm but he is fine otherwise. He wants to speak with you but he is under arrest by the government. If you will keep it a secret, I can pass notes between the two of you."

Ali couldn't believe his ears. "Thank you Lord," he said.

For many days, Ali wrote to Rasheed, sharing his entire story from the dreams to the encounter at the mosque to the encounter with the girl. He shared about the miracles and his new found faith. He wrote about the angel who protected him, and how he felt in his embrace.

Rasheed also wrote Ali about a dream he had had the night before the blast. In it, Rasheed was covered in flames, burning with pain. He saw Ali touch him and the flames were extinguished. Ali introduced him to a man covered in light. He said his name was Isa, and he was our Healer and Savior.

Rasheed awoke from the dream and thought he saw someone in the room but the figure vanished.

Rasheed asked his friend, "Why were these things shown to you? Why do the angels protect you?"

Ali could only answer that he did not know why. It was a mystery to him too.

The nurse destroyed the notes so there would be no evidence against Ali.

When Ali was released from the hospital, he was transferred to a secret prison where he was interrogated on a continual basis. He fell back into his training of total silence. Within a few months, the CIA brought in experts in interrogation to break him down. They spent many hours asking questions. He had committed no crime but they wanted to know why he was there. After numerous attempts to crack his hardened shell of resistance, they gave up and kept him for another week at the prison.

Ali spent many hours in silent prayer while locked in his cell. One night, while not sleeping well, he received a visitor. A light came into the cell. Everyone else stayed asleep. Ali squinted from its brightness. As the light subsided, Trojol, dressed in white, stood before Ali, smiling and saying nothing. Ali asked him, "Who are you? Why are you here? Why have you come?" Ali lips quivered as he spoke.

"Don't be afraid. I am Trojol. I am a messenger from heaven. I have followed you and have protected you. I am making a way for you to complete your task. In 30 days, great judgment will fall on those you served while in your days of darkness. I will open a door for you to go to them and share your story. There will be few who will respond to your message, and many others who will reject it. The Father has heard your prayer to grant mercy to them. Tomorrow, you will be released from this prison. You will meet a farmer at the prison gate. He will take you to the mountains where you will hike into Pakistan. You will have 30 days. When Michael comes, judgment will come swiftly. When they try to kill you, you will be protected. Do not worry. I am sent to follow you." The light rose up and disappeared. Ali laid down and slept soundly for the remainder of the night, his heart filled with wonder.

The next morning, as promised, Ali was released without explanation. When he left the prison compound, he noticed a pickup truck sitting beside the gate. The aged owner stared him down. Ali called out in Pashtun, "Can you give me a ride?" The man nodded, and Ali got in the truck. There was no mention of where or when. This farmer seemed to know every short cut. As night approached, he could see the Tora Bora Mountains in the background. During the long trip, Ali would drift off to sleep.

Just after dawn, Ali was dropped off in the shadow of the mountains. The man handed Ali plenty of water and supplies. Covered by peace, he started the rest of his journey on foot. The farmer smiled and waved goodbye. As Ali walked in the early morning light, he could see a walking path leading through the mountains. The climb was difficult but he felt a sense of direction he couldn't understand. When his strength gave out, he would find a place to rest.

The majesty of the mountains filled his thoughts as he prayed for guidance. He never felt alone. The guidance of the Holy Spirit brought him comfort and direction. He paused to give thanks for the change in his life, its new purpose and meaning. The once gaping emptiness was filled with immeasurable joy.

During the afternoon heat of the third day, he found a cave. Being exhausted, he laid down for a nap. A deep sleep enveloped him. As he began to dream, he was jolted awake by the butt of a rifle. He opened his eyes to see himself surrounded by a group of Al-Qaeda warriors. They spoke Pashtun, "Why are you here? Who are you? Are you a spy? Why should we not kill you?"

"I am Ali Hassan. I trained here in Afghanistan for many years. I am here to fulfill my mission. I stayed in Jordan for many years to set up a source of supply for you. I did not receive any support or directions. I found a relief organization that would sell me food and supplies. But I know that everything has changed. I am here to help in any way I can."

"You lie. You are a spy for the Americans," one of them shouted.

"No, wait. I know him," spoke one of the soldiers.

"He did train here. He is one of us," said another high ranking member. However, no one could remember what his assignment was or who gave the orders. Ali knew that God had made a way for him. While some of the leaders mistrusted him, others welcomed him.

He was allowed to stay with them, but since there was still caution among the leaders, Ali was not privy to any meetings and was never shown where the weapons were kept. The men shared many stories of battles and lost comrades. Their faces were tired and gaunt. They had suffered tremendously. They had food but it was hard to come by. Every other month, a small group would venture out into Pakistan to find more.

Ali shared some of his stories of Jordan and how he came to find this cave. The soldiers were amazed. Ali held back many of the details, waiting for the right time.

One day while on watch detail, one of the men opened up to him. "Ali, I had a dream about you last week. I was surprised to see you. In the dream, you told me that you had met a man named Isa. He heals the sick and raises the dead. He comes to us and says that we should believe in Him and His love. You said that He is our Savior. I told you "No" in the dream. After that, a bright light appeared in the room. I felt a warm love and kindness fill the place. I heard you say that He loves us and we must come to Him. I came closer to the light and the feelings of love grew so strong. I had no power to resist. Then I woke up and I was covered in sweat. I looked up and saw a man dressed in white. He asked me not to tell anyone about the dream until the time was right. He then disappeared right in front of me. You are the first person I have told. If I speak of this with the leaders, they will kill me. I am so afraid but every time I think of that light, I feel strong."

Ali knew the Lord had thrown open a door for him. He shared for hours the parts of his story that he had hidden from the others. The two men soon knew each other as brothers in a completely new way. They agreed to continue to meet in secret.

The days of Ali's semi-captivity flew by. There had been very little action in the soldier's region. There had a small fire fight when one of the teams went on a food run. They were surprised by a patrol of Pakistani soldiers. They escaped but it made the leader paranoid. They felt that the food runs were being watched. They changed some of the paths and started going to a different village to get food.

Meanwhile, the clandestine meetings with Ali grew. One by one, soldiers came to Ali to secretly discuss their dreams. Within three weeks of Ali's arrival, 10 men had found Isa and His love.

At the same time, the leaders started becoming more erratic. They discussed moving the base but said some would have to stay here. They had heard whispers of secret meetings going on but Ali was never questioned about it. However, Ali knew that his time was short and they would soon know everything. He could see it in their eyes every time they ate together.

At the dawn of the twenty ninth day, Ali was startled from his sleep. The butt of a rifle sunk into his rib cage. "What are you doing?" Ali shouted in a stupor.

"You will see," the gun man answered. Ali was gruffly hoisted by one of his fellow soldiers and led into the cave where the leaders met in secret. They tied ropes around his hands and feet.

Through the darkness, he saw the other members of his secret meetings—his fellow believers. The main leader stepped up to Ali and shouted, "Why do you blaspheme Allah in this place? You have led astray Allah's warriors. For this you will die."

There was no trial, no witnesses, and no jury. It was the leader's sole decision. Who had betrayed him, Ali did not know. Nor did he know the fate of the other believers.

Four soldiers stepped forward with rifles in their hands. Raising the barrels to take aim, Ali saw the tears running down their faces. They were crying for the man they loved. The leader spoke the command and the cave rang with sound of the rifles releasing their projectiles. Bullets ripped through Ali's flesh. He fell to the floor of the cave. As the blood continued flowing, he clung to life as his spirit rose. He could see his lifeless body below him. He hovered over it for 15 minutes as he watched the men throw his body in a box. Then the men grabbed shovels and began digging. Suddenly, an angel grabbed Ali by the hand and said, "You must go back. Ten men need you right now. His messengers will show you what to do." Without waiting for an answer, the angel took Ali's hand and returned him to the lifeless, bullet-riddled body in the casket.

When Ali awoke, everything was dark. He tried to move but he was trapped. He raised his head a few inches before it struck the wood of the casket lid. He moved his hands to the side. It was wood also. His feet felt the same. Ali realized with a start that he was inside the casket. It brought a sense of fear he had never known. Then reasoning kicked in. *Why would God send me back to a casket just to die again?* As the minutes expired and all of his efforts to raise the lid failed, Ali cried out, hearing nothing for his efforts but a muffled silence. A countdown of sorts appeared in Ali's head as his oxygen supply grew depleted. Then a whisper entered the darkness. "Michael is coming."

"What does that mean?" Ali yelled out.

"You will see," the voice said before everything returned to silence.

Ali put his faith in the Almighty who was strong to rescue. As he smiled, the ground started to shake. He felt movement. The buried casket was hoisted out of its grave with incredible speed. The lid flew open and darkness fled the blinding light.

When Ali could finally focus, he had trouble believing what his eyes were showing him. There stood an angel—an archangel. Its size was magnificent—at least 20 feet tall. He was rounding up Ali's ten fellow believers.

After regaining his breath from the casket, Ali tried to walk but could only wobble, weakened at the sight of the heavenly being. The angel led Ali and his Isa-believing companions out of the cave and across the mountains. Apparently, they were well hidden because American Drones flew straight over them but never attacked. Instead, the drones seemed headed straight for the cave where Ali had been held. Time had run out for the others in their group—judgment had come, as the voice had said.

Michael marched with Ali and his companions for many miles, walking them straight into an American Army base and the officers mess tent. As they appeared in the tent, none of the officers seemed to even notice. Then a voice rang out, "Hey, what are you all doing in here?" A guard had noticed them. Ali and his friends froze, not knowing what to answer.

"They are with me," someone said. They all turned to see an American General with dozens of medals and ribbons on his uniform. The name tag read General Trojol. His hair was crew cut and his eyes were blue. "These men are informants and very important to the mission. I felt they deserved a hot meal," he said sternly.

"Very well, sir. My apologies. Get in line, boys, and dig in."

The group cautiously ate the best meal they had had in months. The "General" then took them to the refugee camp in Kandahar and set them free.

Chapter 15
All Together Now

Jennifer's knees trembled as she boarded the jet. It was her first time out of the country, and to be travelling to such a dangerous place as Afghanistan had her nerves on edge. She sighed as she reminded herself it was the right direction for her. She had developed her skills in bringing comfort to those in trauma. Her abilities would be desperately needed in such a war weary region of the globe.

She was leaving behind her friends, family, and the patients that she had grown to love. She clutched her passport and the farewell card they had sent. As she looked out the window at the huge wing of the aircraft, she thought of how God had carried her through so many difficulties. She shuddered when she thought of how close she had come to suicide, and yet there was such an amazing life on the other side of her sorrow.

An African-American woman sat down next to Jennifer. She was a bit overweight and loud. "Stewardess, is it OK if no one sits between me and this woman?" the stout woman said.

Before the response came, the woman corrected herself. "I guess you're called flight attendants now. My bad. Well, can you answer my question here?"

Jennifer was a little embarrassed by her outspokenness.

The flight attendants, realizing that no one would want to sit between those two for obvious reasons, gladly complied, saving themselves of relocating another passenger later in the flight. "That seat will be empty for the entire flight, ma'am. Is there anything else we can help you with before we take off?"

"No, thank you for your hospitality. You do a great job here on this airplane," she said. The attendants nodded, hiding their smirks behind professional, plastic smiles.

"Hi, I'm Mable. Did you want to trade seats?" she said to Jennifer.

"No, I'm fine," replied Jennifer.

"You look a little nervous. Are you sure you are fine?" "Well, this is my first time out of the country," Jennifer replied.

"My honey-child, I have just the thing for you–a pillow and a blanket. They will put you off to sleep in a jiffy. You won't know what hit you."

Mable handed off the gifts. Being polite, Jennifer accepted the sleep aides.

As promised, Jennifer didn't know what hit her. She fell into a deep sleep within moments of takeoff, slipping into another world full of beauty, a place of gardens, waterfalls, mountains, and green vegetation with splotches of brilliant color splattered across a gorgeous landscape. The ground was both dark and soft under her bare feet. Birds sang rapturous melodies and small creatures she had never seen filled the trees with welcoming smiles. *Must be Eden*, she thought. It was awe-inspiring. She turned her gaze towards the sky; a breathtaking blue color laced rolling clouds. She smiled but couldn't stay still. Her curiosity and excitement drove her to continue the exploration of this new world.

Meanwhile, Tom rested heavily in his tent. He was exhausted both physically and emotionally from the long day of hard work. He had spent his day helping others and was looking forward to the relief of a good night's rest. *I guess I have lived a rich and comfortable life compared to these people. They have lost everything. At least I'm giving something back. I never knew this much suffering existed.*

Tom was asleep and dreaming as his head hit the rag pillow. In a blink of an eye, he had left war-torn Afghanistan and entered a dream so beautiful, he thought it was the Garden of Eden. Tom, who had been so tired while awake, was now full of energy. He took off running and leaping, laughing and singing as he bounded through the garden. Then without warning, he crashed into an invisible wall with a thud. It wasn't a painful collision but it was a shock. He stood up and retraced his steps, finally finding it—an invisible wall that seemed like thick plastic sheet separating him from the other side of the garden.

Then he saw someone on the other side of the wall–a very beautiful girl who apparently also saw him from a distance. Her eyes penetrated his soul. Her hair blew softly in the breeze. His heart started to pound. There was something about this girl, yet they had never met before. It was like she knew him and he knew her. She seemed to read his very thoughts as he could read hers.

She strode to the barrier with a warm and confident smile, reaching out her hand to touch the wall. Tom placed his hand in the same place as hers, finger tip to finger tip. Though separated, warmth transferred through the invisible barrier. They could feel each other's heart beat.

As Tom's excitement grew to a fevered pitch, a hand touched his shoulder. It startled him awake. Charlie was waking him to tell him they had to go into town to do some errands for the relief effort.

"Why did you wake me up?" Tom snapped.

"Because you overslept. But you seemed to be enjoying yourself," Charlie said with a grin.

"Well, it was an awesome dream. There was this girl…" Tom began wistfully.

"Look, we have no time to talk about the girl of your dreams. We have a lot of work to do right now," Charlie replied.

"It was innocent. I mean, she was so beautiful. I could feel her touch. It was amazing," Tom said dreamily.

"It doesn't sound innocent to me. It sounds like you have it bad for her. We don't have time for this."

They both laughed as Charlie continued.

"Stay away from women, Tom Johnson. They'll get you into trouble every time. Look what happened to Adam, Samson, and don't forget… ah, what's the use.

"You seem to worry about my love life or lack thereof way too much," Tom retorted.

"I guess it's OK to dream, but I'm not losing my best friend to fleeting romance. Not when we have so much to do. Get dressed. I'm not going to wait all day. You've already slept through half of it," snapped Charlie, half in jest.

"Miss, you need to wake up. The plane is landing. You will have to buckle up," said the flight attendant. As Jennifer opened her eyes, she noticed her hands were still fully extended into the row in front of her as if she was touching the invisible wall. She buckled in and tried to hide the embarrassment from what she might have said or done in her sleep. She glanced over at the woman sitting next to her, hoping she didn't notice anything. She was praying for some quietness and discretion. Her boisterous neighbor demonstrated neither.

"Honey child, whatever you were dreaming about, if you could package it and sell it…whoo-wee! You'd be the richest woman in Georgia. The look on your face was pure heaven."

The other passengers around her broke out in laughter.

"I hope I didn't embarrass you," Mable continued, "but you were having some kind of dream. And if no one has told you, you are one beautiful woman. It is so good to see you again, Jennifer Hill."

As Jennifer blushed and glanced away, the woman vanished. This seemed especially unusual considering that the plane was still taxiing to the tarmac. All the passengers were still buckled in.

"Sir, did you see where the woman who was sitting next to me went?" Jennifer asked the flight attendant.

"I'm sorry, ma'am. Which woman?" she answered.

"The one that was sitting next to me in this row," Jennifer said.

"I'm sorry. Those seats have been empty the entire flight. Can you describe her?" asked the attendant.

"Yes, she was African-American, had a southern accent, she was a little over weight, and…ah, never mind." Jennifer said as another thought crept slowly into her mind.

"I'm sorry, miss. There are no passengers like that on this plane. Perhaps you have this flight confused with your previous connecting flight. You did sleep the entire time."

"Yes, perhaps you are right," Jennifer conceded. She sat puzzled again just like when she was whisked away from the burning car, or found herself in the hospital after the mysterious chaplain gave her the mirror. She was smart enough to know not to ask any more questions about this woman. *Why did she say nice to see you again and then knew my name. I never told her.* Then a huge grin broke on her face as the realization set in. *An angel brought me a dream from God. I wonder what it means.*

Once in Kandahar, she travelled with a group providing medical care to the refugees in various areas. After arrival, she set up her tent and examined the busy schedule set up for her at the camp. Her first task was to travel from tent to tent, passing out vitamins, basic medicine, and hygiene supplies. Although she was not a doctor or a nurse, her work in the hospital had prepared her to be a help in the mobile clinic.

Since the Afghan women were very apprehensive about receiving help from men, female relief workers were very useful in aiding the women in a variety of ways. Jennifer starting helping an eight year old girl by taking out her stitches. The little girl was excited about meeting this "foreigner." She looked Jennifer over and wanted to compare the size of their hands. They placed their hands together and tried to reach finger tip to finger tip. The girl's hands were much smaller and one of her fingers was not straight. It must have been broken when she was much younger and not properly set.

As if by pre-arrangement, Tom and Charlie were passing down the same street and Tom saw Jennifer. The finger tip touching triggered his memory of the dream. But instead of rushing to meet the woman of his dreams, he panicked, grabbing Charlie and ducking behind a tent.

"What are you doing?" Charlie asked.

"It's her," he said.

"Who? What are you talking about?"

"The girl I saw in the dream. It's her. I swear that it is the exact same girl."

"Oh yeah, the dream girl. Of course," mused Charlie.

"Shut up," Tom shot back, then regretted it. "I'm sorry, Charlie. I mean, what do I do? This is crazy. That is the same girl. Honest!"

"Maybe you should introduce yourself to her. 'Hi. I'm Tom – your dream man.' That's a good start, don't you think?" Charlie said with a smirk on his face.

"This is no time to be funny. Look at me. My hair is nasty. I haven't changed clothes in a week. Who knows how I smell? I haven't even shaved," Tom complained.

"I know how you smell—trust me. Besides, the hair gives you that rugged look. Chicks dig the Marlboro Man. Maybe one of refugees could loan you a smoke," Charlie joked.

"Stop it. Now you are making me laugh. And this is serious," said Tom, failing to suppress a grin.

"Get over there, Casanova," Charlie said as he shoved Tom into the open. "If you don't introduce yourself, I will."

"I'm going to get you for this," Tom said.

"As long as it doesn't involve a car, I'll be ok," Charlie laughed.

"It will definitively involve a car," Tom replied. "I am just going to walk right by and act like nothing is going on."

"Ok, I dare you."

As Tom came from behind the tent, Jennifer popped out from the other direction. Their eyes met and time froze on the arid landscape of Afghanistan. Jennifer gasped. *That's the same man who was in my dream. I look terrible. Oh, my hair. And I haven't changed these clothes since I got here.*

None of this mattered, however, as they continued to stare at each other with a strange and awkward silence. The young girl took her fingertips off Jennifer's hand and put Tom's hand in her place. She did the same with their other hands, and giggled as she skipped across the compound to find her mother.

Tom couldn't stop staring into Jennifer's eyes. Yes, it was the same captivating eyes, the same expression of wonder on her face, and even the same reflection of sunlight on her hair.

Jennifer stood frozen yet never felt more alive. There were those eyes that could penetrate into her very soul. She saw a greater strength, a greater confidence, a man of depth. She didn't know how she knew this but she did. It was as though the secrets of their hearts were being transmitted through their touch (or maybe an angel was playing matchmaker—stranger things had happened to both of them).

A dusty refugee center is not rated as one of the top ten places to fall in love, but it was happening here. In the midst of the chaos and sorrow, disruption and death, an amazing love and joy was springing forth. As their individual discovery of God's love had come amidst great pain and difficulty, so was the birth of their mutual love—an encore performance of God's magnificent redeeming grace.

Right on cue, a light breeze started to blow. Only this breeze was different. Normally, the wind on the plains of Afghanistan blows straight, but this time it swirled around the new couple like a small hurricane. They stood in the storm's eye as fierce dust clouds howled about them. Someone was putting their supernatural seal of approval on this relationship. In time, the wind died down and the silence was broken. They started to talk, curious about each other, like... names. They soon discovered that they were inseparable. They always had something (and Someone) to talk about. They connected on so many levels. They shared their stories, their hearts, and their God.

Chapter 16
The Finale

Tom, Charlie, and Jennifer found that they worked well as a team, so they stayed together and were able to pray for a lot of hurting people. Unfortunately, the turmoil around them increased as the miracles increased. They started to get death threats and warnings, yet they supported each other and did not quit.

One night as Charlie and Tom slept; they were aroused by the sound of conversation. Tom got up and looked outside to see what was going on. Charlie told him to wait a minute. Within seconds, a hailstorm of rocks and sticks struck their tent. They hit the dirt and rolled under their cots as their tent fell to the ground. Three or four men ran onto the fallen tent and tried to stomp them. Whistles started to blow, scaring the attackers away. The compound security forces chased the men, who disappeared into the night. Tom and Charlie spent the remainder of the night with the compound director.

The next day, they repaired their tent and picked up the mess. Some of the rocks had messages like, "Witches go home," and "Death to the infidels." From the then on, American soldiers patrolled the camp, which only added to the tension.

The nightly sneak attacks continued and no one ever was caught. Tom and Charlie resorted to moving their tent to a more remote area and changing their routine to not be a target.

Things took a turn for the worse when they started caring for a local man named Ali Hassan, who had walked into the compound. He was very bold in his faith, speaking of angels and the healing power of Isa or Jesus.

After Ali told them about his dreams, his experiences, and his unusual scar on his chest, Tom and Charlie also shared their journey with the Lord. It wasn't long before they were friends.

Ali's presence also became a magnet for Al Qaida, who wanted to kill him. He was a prime target—maximum terror potential—and the tension escalated.

One night as the camp director was preaching to the volunteers, he spoke about fire. As Charlie listened to the sermon, a chill ran down his spine. From his experiences as a child, fire symbolized everything he feared. It meant death, destruction, being cut-off from love. It had destroyed his peaceful childhood and took the life of the dearest person in his world—his mom. Fire haunted him in his dreams. The mere sight of it brought back those terrible memories—nowhere to run, nowhere to hide. But this sermon forced him to see fire in a new way.

The director taught that God uses fire to purify. It burns away the chaff of everything unneeded and unwanted. Indeed, this fire was from the Holy Spirit; it was unquenchable. It fostered deep passion and brought clarity to a desperately seeking world. Although the fire Charlie remembered was bent on destroying him, God changed his paradigm. Charlie now saw fire as forging him, purifying him, molding him into something amazing, someone that even God would be proud of, enabling him to display God's splendor in a dark world.

The sermon on fire also drove a stake in Jennifer's heart. Despite the fact that her fire was her own doing, its purpose was to destroy many things in her life: her beauty, her self-worth, her life, and the lives of those around her.

Instead, the God of the universe created a new Jennifer, starting from the inside out. She had always focused inward to see her pain and problems. Now she focused outward, seeing the needs of others. In the process, a new Jennifer came forth. This new person had a joy that could not be contained. It bubbled over to everyone she met.

As the sermon continued, the speaker read from Hebrews chapter 11—a remembrance of the founders of the faith—and noted that some had surrendered their bodies to flames. A big tear fell on Charlie's Bible. He put a tight lid on his emotions. How could anyone surrender their body to flames? It would be such a grotesque and painful way to die. But in a way, his heart had already started down this path.

Sometimes, surrendering to the flames meant surrendering to God's passion instead of our own. God's passion is to restore, to heal, to help, and to love. Charlie had indeed surrendered to this. That night, everyone listening to this message pondered these things, but one would be called to live it.

The next day was hot and windy—not unusual for Afghanistan. It was also going to be another tough day for the volunteers. There were so many needs and so few supplies. Ali went into town with Jennifer and a few others to check on a shipment. Charlie and Tom slept-in, which proved to be a costly mistake. Upon waking late, Tom stepped out of his tent to encounter fifteen heavily armed men in ambush. They forced him and Charlie into a car and sped off. Charlie looked out the window with a strange longing to tell everyone goodbye.

The camp director saw the commotion in the distance and called for the US Army soldiers to assist. Even with their trained preparedness, they arrived too late, rolling into the camp as the dust was settling from the kidnappers' car. Ali and Jennifer pulled into camp at the same time. Against the officer's orders, Jennifer jumped in one of the Humvees with the soldiers as they gave chase to the terrorists' vehicle.

The kidnappers drove until late in the night, to a village where they had greater control. They pulled into a concealed garage and changed vehicles. Because the army's Humvees were slowed by sniper fire, they arrived at the village late and could see no trace of the kidnappers. The army conducted a house-to-house sweep to find them. They put a bullet proof vest on Jennifer, even as they tried to dissuade her from accompanying them. Their words had no effect; her stubborn streak had come alive. In Jesus name.

The terrorists pulled Tom and Charlie, still bound, from the car and into an old Soviet-style military vehicle. They threw cans of fuel into the back. One of the containers did not have the top screwed on properly, and its contents spilled all over the bed of the vehicle, filling the air with the gasoline vapors.

The terrorist leader screamed at his men for the mishap. Despite the tirade, they knocked it over again and the puddles got deeper.

"God, please get the army here in time," Tom prayed.

Charlie was also focused in prayer. "God, deliver Tom from their hands. I know the plans you have for him. Whatever you ask of me, I am willing. Only, spare Tom, that he may live to fulfill your purpose."

As the soldiers approached the kidnappers" house, the lookout spotted them and a firefight ensued. Alert to the danger of the spilled gasoline, Tom cried out, "No!" The soldiers heard Tom's voice, misunderstood, and started shooting at the windows. Tom managed to roll out of the truck but was still bound. He called for Charlie, who merely looked at Tom and said firmly, "Run." A flash grenade was thrown inside, igniting the gasoline. The flames rose quickly around the serenely calm Charlie.

As Tom's hands were still bound, he could do nothing but cry out. Charlie's body was quickly covered in flames. One of the terrorists jumped into the driver's seat, drove the vehicle through the garage door, and was gunned down by the American forces as he tried to drive away. The burning vehicle stopped in the street with its contents rapidly being consumed.

As the ropes burned away, Charlie lifted his hands to heaven and started praising God. He felt no pain from the fire. The terrified villagers watched from their hideouts as the surrounded terrorists laid down their weapons. An American soldier quickly ran to the vehicle with a fire extinguisher, struggling to put down the flames. A badly burned Charlie continued to praise God.

Tom ran to his friend as the flames went out. "Charlie, you're going to make it. Just hold on," he screamed.

"Tom, I see heaven and it's so beautiful. Trojol is waiting for me. Goodbye my friend," Charlie said with his last breath.

Tom knelt down and cried as Jennifer ran to him. They couldn't believe he was dead. Tom reached for Jennifer and held her. The tears flowed down Tom's dust covered cheeks and onto her matted hair.

The soldiers had rounded up the rest of the kidnappers, and were wrapping up Charlie's body. As they laid it in a Humvee, Tom said, "Goodbye my friend, see you in heaven."

The impact of Charlie's death on Tom was devastating. He had to inform David and Aunt Bev, then arrange to have his body flown back to the US. As Tom pondered all of the memories that they shared together, he felt haunted. Charlie's gruesome ending overshadowed the intense joy of their fellowship and ministry.

For Tom, the questions never stopped. *Couldn't God have stopped this?* Tom considered Charlie one of the most awesome people he had ever known–impossible to replace. The world became a darker place without him. His anguish turned inward into the dark night of his wandering soul.

Tom began to have trouble with the basic elements of life as his depression grew. He couldn't sleep, eat, or even think clearly. Hope drained from him like a whirlpool of despair. The only thing he could taste was bitterness, for his life had become like a lemon soaked in vinegar. Everything tasted that way. Everything smelled that way.

Jennifer helped as much as she could. She was a Godsend in so many ways. Her gentleness and patience was the balm that enabled Tom's short-term survival. She flew with him back home. She drove him to Sharpsville and met with Aunt Bev and David.

Although he couldn't feel it, God was indeed with Tom in his despair, and God was about to make himself known in a new way.

While arranging for the funeral, Jennifer called Bill. She found out he'd been transferred to the hospital.

"He's not expected to live the night," the nurse told her. Tom and Jennifer rushed to the hospital, only to find that they were too late. Bill had passed away; Tom never got to say goodbye. He laid in the floor and wept again, grieved by the thought of his broken promise to be there when he died. Jennifer held him as his eyes failed to find more tears. His wounds were too deep to cry through anymore. They were too deep to be angry. He had nothing left.

The funerals came and went. There was no resurrection, no great miracles, no 21-gun salute. Just a few friends who knew and loved them.

Charlie was buried beside his mother. *How ironic that he and his mother both died in the same way*, thought Tom. *It was like a destiny of fire followed him his entire life.*

For a brief moment, Tom felt something. It was anger. Then it turned inward to where his other emotions were buried. "It doesn't matter," Tom said to himself. He was unable to speak at the funeral. He was unable to articulate the amazing person Charlie was, or the amazing person Bill was.

Where is the Reverend R.J. Drakes? Where is Billy Owens? The resurrection had propelled them both into international notoriety. But Charlie got nothing for it. No thank-you, no hugs, no television interviews, nothing but obscurity. Where are the TV cameras now?

Tom's anger raged. *What's the use?*

There was a cold rain the day Bill's body was put in the ground. He was buried behind the old church—the very one Tom had seen in the dream an eternity ago. The gray skies and soggy ground matched how Tom felt. *At least the weather mourns for my friend*, he thought.

Later that day, he sat in a hotel room, his mind and heart shut off to the world. As he meditated on the nothingness, he felt a presence enter the room. He could feel someone to the right of him though he could not see him. He started to feel something again, beginning with anger. "I guess I can't hope that you will go away?" he said to his invisible friend. Light filled the room. He now saw Trojol sitting beside him. There was a long silence. Tom looked at him and said, "I'm not doing any assignments right now. Can't you see what just happened here?"

More silence. Then Trojol finally spoke. "I'm not here to give you an assignment."

"Then, what are you here for?" Tom shouted in anger.

"I'm here to comfort you. Come with me," Trojol said with a knowing smile.

"Just leave me alone," Tom said as he started to cry.

"I brought someone with me. Do you remember me talking about the encouraging angel?" asked Trojol.

"Well, no one in heaven or earth could encourage me right now," he shot back.

"I betcha he can," said Trojol, still sporting his smile.

"Don't play with me," demanded Tom.

"I'm not going to do that. I have my orders you know," replied Trojol.

"You're impossible. This is like arguing with an angel. Alright, where is he? Let's get this over with," Tom said as he wiped his puffy eyes.

As Tom turned his head, there was nothing and Trojol was gone.

"Great, you're playing a joke on me. Well, I'm glad you're gone. Just stay gone," Tom screamed.

"No, I assure you he is here," a voice rang out. Tom recalled that he could see nothing without faith, when suddenly his eyes opened. The encouraging angel had straight dark hair, very different from Trojol's dark curly hair. However, their eyes were similar–the brightest blue he had ever seen.

"I see you now. Go ahead. Tell me what you came here for," Tom said as he hung his head.

"I know why you are angry. I have seen it. I saw Charlie's life. I saw Bill's life. They were greatly pleasing to the Father. I am going to show you something that will completely change your perspective on their deaths. First of all, the Father knows your pain because He feels it even now. In fact, the pain he endures for His children is beyond what you could ever experience. Do you remember the Bible story of Jesus in the garden of Gethsemane?" the angel asked.

"Yeah, where he sweated a lot and an angel strengthened him. Then he got captured and went to the cross. Why do you ask?"

"That's right. I was that angel. I strengthened Him. I encouraged Him in the garden. But it was very different than you pictured. It wasn't the first time I had encouraged and strengthened Him. It was such a privilege for me to see Him and speak with Him. Whenever I approached Him, I felt what he felt. The burdens he bore were beyond description. Few will ever understand the depths of his love and sacrifice. In his toughest times, he drew all of the strength I had come to give Him from the Father. I was glad to serve my Lord in such circumstances.

But that night in the garden, I had never seen him that way. I knew how drained he got when he had to confront Satan directly. But this was different. What was happening to Him, the Devil could not do. The weight of the world was on his shoulders. He had no strength of his own, but he wasn't drawing any strength from me. He was asking the Father for another way. I was so used to seeing Him on the throne filled with all majesty and power. This was heartbreaking for me. I was speechless. I felt that I had nothing to say, nothing I could do as he sat there in despair. My very presence was confirmation that there was no other way. He knew I was there to help Him cope with the anguish ahead, but still he petitioned the Father for another way.

Then as I sat in bewilderment, a curious thing happened. The Dove hovered over both of us. I felt the Spirit's urge to speak. As I opened my mouth, all that was given me was a simple name of one of His followers. The Spirit started showing Jesus the willing sacrifice of that follower's life for him. Jesus could hear her say "I Love You, Jesus." She laid down her life for him. This moved Him.

Another name was given me and I spoke it out. Again, the Spirit showed Jesus the life of this saint—his love and devotion, his trials and struggles, and finally his ultimate redemption.

Soon, the names were coming so fast that Jesus had to go beyond the realm of time to see them all. It lasted for weeks, months, years. No one knows; only God knows. But Jesus saw them all. Some made small sacrifices, some large, some gave Him their all. Charlie Harris was one who gave everything. Jesus took special courage from Charlie's life and death. It encouraged our Savior. It brought strength to Him. He saw Charlie praising God through the flames. It blessed Him.

Jesus' reward for the cross was the people he would save. It was the joy set before Him. That is how He endured the cross. This was the treasure awaiting Him.

After the displays, He amazed me in a way I never dreamed possible. He stood up and, with a smile on his face, said 'I'm ready, Father, to do your will.' The power of that statement knocked me to the ground. The trees shuddered from its impact. All creatures rejoiced. He stood and walked back to His disciples. He was going to the cross. Nothing was going to stop him. He said, 'I am going to receive my bride prepared for me since the foundation of the earth.' He woke his disciples and faced his accusers.

I don't know how to understand or explain it any better. It was so unlike anything I had ever seen in heaven, before or since."

After a pause, the angel continued, "I have something else to show you, Tom."

"What is that?" asked Tom.

"I have come to show you your friends Charlie and Bill."

"What do you mean?" stammered Tom.

"I am taking you to heaven to see them. I know you are afraid that this means you will never return to the earth. But rest assured, you will be returning right after you are shown what God wants you to know.

You will be joined by Jennifer Hill, Ann Wentworth, and the man Ali whom you know very little about now, but he will be a replacement for Charlie in many ways. His full name is Ali Hassan. Come with me, now."

He directed Tom to a small horseless chariot nearby. They climbed aboard and within seconds, they were approaching heaven. Its beauty was beyond Tom's comprehension. His friends were at the gates of pearl–the entrance to heaven. Tom now understood why his companion was called the "encouraging angel." He was enjoying the new perspective. Many of the difficult times in his life were coming into perspective. What he thought were horrible tragedies, were in fact the threads of a master weaver. Even his nightmares became loving redirections that would have never gained his attention otherwise. Despite all his failings, they didn't seem to matter anymore. This new revelation was creating a new love in him that would rock his world forever. This new paradigm would change not only him, but many others. It would release an indescribable joy. It would be a new day.

Waiting for Tom's thoughts to subside, the angel finally continued, "The things that you see today, do not tell to anyone until the time is right. Your enemy will try to thwart God's plans for you but he will not prevail. God's purposes for you will stand forever. This day of revelation was planned for you from your birth. Satan tried to stop it many times. God formed a shield of protection for you that could never be undone. Trojol was part of that shield. He has done many things for you through the years. Even when you did not know the Lord or His love, Trojol was standing for you at His command. You are highly favored. Don't take that for granted. Always be thankful."

The encouraging angel paused to let his words sink in. As Tom stepped out of the chariot of fire, there stood Jennifer. She ran to him and they embraced.

"I never dreamed this could happen. Can't you feel the joy and the love in this place? It is contained in every breath I breathe. Everything is so amazing! The colors, the smells, the sights, everything is so beautiful."

Ann and Ali were equally in awe of their new surroundings. Ali felt weak and started to fall. An angel caught him and gave him some fruit from a tree, then passed some to the others.

"Here, this will give all of you strength for the visit," the angel said.

As they ate it, their senses came alive with new sensations. The fruit dissolved in their mouths and never entered their stomach. They felt strength surge to every part of them.

An angel came for Ali first. Ali was so full of questions, but before he could ask anything, the angel spoke, "I know your questions. Many of them will not be answered at this time, but God is aware of them and will answer them in time when you are ready. Although you will understand very little of what is going on around you, be assured of this. God will teach you many things quickly. The time is short. Your brothers will need the message that you will bring to them. The Father has seen your heart. He knows that you are not only willing to die for Him but you are also willing to live for Him. You will be murdered many more times. You will be tortured. You will be rejected, not only by your brothers, but by the world also. You will even be rejected by many who name the name of Christ. But you will not falter. You will be steady and strong. You will fulfill your purpose. You will walk in a love and joy that only the living martyrs can experience.

Judge no one, for some who appear to be your enemy will be your friend. Some who appear to be your friend will betray you and become your enemy. This will happen to reveal the hearts of men. Believe me when I say, your heart will rejoice any time His power flows through you. No one will be able to resist the will of the Father in your life. Love all, and your joy will be complete and His power will be perfected in you."

The angel led him to a large home. It was beautiful and ornate. "There is someone inside who has asked to see you. Your meeting will bring you both great joy." Ali stepped inside to be greeted by his old

Imam. The hand print was still visible through his garment on his chest. They ran and embraced.

"I cannot tell you how happy I am right now," Ali said.

His old friend replied, "I know your joy. I can feel it. It is my joy also. I am even more excited knowing your position in His Kingdom. You have no idea the calling that is on your life. All of heaven is talking about you and your missions. And to think I had a part to play in your rising. It is such a privilege for me."

"I am nothing. I know so little. I cannot understand what you are telling me. You were so kind to me when I was afraid. Knowing that you lost your life helping me, I'm so sorry. I never knew this would happen. You made the ultimate sacrifice for me," Ali said to his old friend.

"It was my choice. The Savior was so pleased with that decision. Many people tell me that they are honored to be with me. It was not only for you. It was for Him. It was my destiny. I fulfilled my purpose. Obey whatever the Father tells you. His reward is so good. It is worth any pain and shame in our earthly life. Our reward is better than life itself," the Imam said to Ali.

They spoke more words of comfort until the angel pulled them apart, saying it was the time to go.

"We will see each other again soon," the Imam said to his friend as the distance began to separate them.

"Goodbye my friend," Ali said.

As Ali turned around, the angel was gone. A mist had surrounded him. Ali looked in all directions. He could see no one. He could see nothing. The questions began to pour through his mind. Without warning, Jesus himself stepped through the fog and stood in front of Ali. Ali's strength left him as he fell. Before he hit the ground, Jesus caught him. Those eyes of blue fire captivated his attention.

"Ali, I first of all want to thank you for serving me. I know it has not been easy. It will get even more difficult. Be at peace. I am with you every step of the way. I am giving you an unusual gift that will open doors that you never dreamed possible. You will stand before kings and princes. You will proclaim my name and my Kingdom. The Holy Spirit will defend you as well as the angels I assign to you. You are mine and I will never let you go. Remember the words the angel told you. They are my words. They are life for you. I will never leave your side."

The words Jesus spoke went right through Ali, bringing joy and pain at the same time. He knew that this was what he had searched for his whole life. This was his dream. As his Savior stood with him, the fog lifted and they were surrounded by millions of others who were dropping to their knees in adoration of their Lord. It was just like his dream. Ali closed his eyes. Instantly, he was transported back to the earth.

The angel came for Jennifer next. He explained that Ali had been taken back to the earth and that they would meet up again. They would travel and minister together but in a way that was not preferred. She was filled with wonder and curiosity.

"Jennifer, you are very important to God's plan for the earth. When you came here, you weren't able to have children because of the accident. However, you did not know this. When you want children, you will have them. That is the Father's promise to you."

Jennifer blushed. She had been secretly hoping for Tom to ask her for her hand in marriage. She somehow now knew the answer to her other question.

The angel continued. "When the time comes, your daughter will be powerful in the Lord. She will also be important in God's plan. Be a good mother for her. There will be few people who will understand her. You will be given a special wisdom for her. The enemy has already found out about her. He will resist her birth. God's promise to you is firm, and it will be fulfilled. She will live and not die but declare God's Glory in all of the earth."

The angel led her away to another area. There was a moderate sized house with toys in the windows. She could tell that a whole family lived here. As she walked, she was greeted by Jeff, his wife and their two children. The angel explained to Jennifer, "This is the man you ministered to in the hospital after your healing. He was suicidal when you met him. The Holy Spirit gave you words for him. This man started going to church after you met him. He soon dedicated his life to helping burn victims in Mexico. He died a martyr's death when his vehicle was attacked by a drug gang. He was rejoined with his family after receiving his crown."

The angel stepped back to let them talk to each other. Jeff embraced his friend.

"I'm so happy to see you here," she said.

"I wouldn't be here if it weren't for you. God used you to save me. You stubbornly believed in me when my guilt was overwhelming. You helped me to see the light when all I saw was darkness. I will always be grateful to you for reaching out to me. I had so much anger and regret. I had no hope. You were my lifeline. Oh, let me introduce you to my family," Jeff said.

A beautiful woman and two children stepped forward. The girls were very young, and bore no sadness. As Jennifer started to explain who she was, the woman stopped her and said, "I know who you are. I am so thankful that God sent you to Jeff. I prayed for him every day until the day I arrived here. God heard my prayers."

The two girls kept pulling on their father's robe, asking the question, "Daddy, is it true that we will be together forever in this place?"

"Yes, it is true. We'll never be apart. It's forever," he said as they squealed in delight. Jennifer realized that the gentle tug on her heart the morning before she met Jeff was the Lord's commanding voice. It would have been so easy to miss.

They soon parted ways as the angel was telling her that more things were awaiting her.

He took her to a large set of warehouses. Inside was a hall where she could not see the end. Shelves lined both sides of the warehouse as a flurry of angels were busy adding things to the shelves. The angel took her to one of the shelves. She was shocked to see human body parts on the shelf with a corresponding name underneath each item. Before she could ask, the angel explained. "Whenever someone on the earth loses a body part, a new one is created and placed here."

Jennifer did some reasoning and interjected. "So when you come to heaven, they will have a new body that's whole. Right?"

There was a pause as the angel resounded with, "No, that is not correct. This is to restore the body part to the person while they are on the earth. All they have to do is claim it. Under assignment, an angel can bring it to them through a person who has interceded for them. You are being shown this for a reason. You will teach people this truth. I came a few years ago to this spot to retrieve something for you." She looked and saw her name on a shelf. There was nothing there but she could tell something had once been there. She asked about it.

"When you were in that fire, even before you started to burn, new skin and hair was placed here. Someone interceded for you and they claimed your skin and hair. They did not understand what they were doing or who they were praying for, but they obeyed. That is why obedience is so important to God. You will learn this in a new way.

There is one more thing that you must learn. You are going to be given a gift. You must be faithful with it. You will begin to feel in your body the pain or affliction of another. You must intercede for them. You must press through. Your faith must be activated. This is God's intercession through you. He knows all and He feels all. You must collaborate with Him in this endeavor, for it is pleasing to Him. Sometimes you will know who it is and sometimes you will not. You must pray, for God has given you healing hands and a healing heart. This anointing will grow in you if you stay faithful to it. It will bear much fruit and reap many rewards."

Immediately, Jennifer and the angel were back to the gates of pearl. "You must travel back to the earth with Tom. He will have an important question for you. It is your heart's desire. You have already foreseen this for it has been in your dreams."

The angel then grabbed Ann's hand. "You must come with me,"

he said. Ann was used to being the one in charge and barking out the commands. Still, in this wondrous place, she adapted quickly to be an obedient servant. From the moment the angel touched her, she knew who she was going to see. The anticipation was building. She was led to a large home. They walked through into an expansive courtyard around which the house was built. There stood a beautiful fountain. It was unlike anything she had ever seen before. She could feel the water praising God.

As she adored the ornate stone work, she heard a faintly familiar voice, "Mom?" She turned around to greet her daughter. They embraced for what seemed like a month. The rapturous joy was felt by both. No words were needed. As soon as Ann would try to talk, her daughter would say, "I know." They looked at each other and laughed uncontrollably. A bell rang out like the school bells on the earth. Within seconds, hundreds of children flooded into the courtyard.

To Ann's surprise, they were all coming to see her. One after another ran to her and hugged her. With each child, a strange phenomenon would occur during the embrace. It was like a supernatural download of information about the child entered her mind. Everything from where they were conceived, how they died, their favorite color, their favorite activity, the way they looked, their parents names, all of it flashed before her eyes and imprinted to her memory.

The angel explained. "These children have never seen their parents. They either died in abortion or miscarriage. You will meet their parents and tell them that they are here and they are being cared for. These children, like your daughter, all love their parents deeply. They desperately want to have their parents here with them. Don't worry, Ann. God will prepare the way for you to speak to them just as you were prepared to meet your daughter for the first time. You will go and tell them their children are waiting for them. He is a merciful and loving God. He is reaching out to them in love and so are their children."

Ann was overwhelmed by the love of these children. She bent

down to look into the face of what appeared to be a three year old girl. "Can you tell my mommy and daddy that I love them? Can you give them my teddy bear?" she said while flashing the most beautiful green eyes Ann had ever seen before. Ann reached out for the bear, not expecting the child's love to be encapsulated on it. Ann shook with its power. She was held speechless. She wasn't even able to say "yes" before the child discerned her thoughts and said, "Thank you."

The angel said, "It is time to go." Thousands of children had formed a large crowd around her. Ann's daughter waved goodbye, but Ann knew they would see each other again soon. The children also waved as the angel whisked her away. Ann realized there was one thing missing. She had never given her daughter a name. As she scrambled in her mind for a name, the angel looked at her and said, "Very well, she will be named that."

"What did I name her?" Ann asked, knowing she had thought of dozens of names.

"Ann, you named her Hope. It is a fitting name for her. Hope will visit you many times in your dreams," the angel said.

Within a blink of an eye, Ann was back in her home, sitting at her desk with the Bible opened to this verse. "For the hope which is laid up for you in heaven," (Col 1:5). A big teardrop of thankfulness struck the page as Ann sat speechless. She turned her glance to see the teddy bear resting there in her hand. She smiled, knowing her new mission had begun.

When the angel arrived again at the gates of pearl, Tom knew it was his turn. His emotions had changed from despair to hope, even though he didn't know what was coming. The angel spoke to him, "God has been pursuing you your entire life. He will never give up on you. He has planned so many things for you. You only see what you are and what you were. He sees who you will become. More difficulties and suffering will come to you, but fear not, these things will only help to purify your heart and keep you walking in humility. Never seek fame, for it is a snare. Never seek riches. He will provide for you with abundance. Some men, wanting to control you, will offer you large sums of money. You shall refuse them. You will continue to work with Ann.

You will have to lay your life down repeatedly. Yet you will find a life that is better than your wildest dreams. Charlie has modeled a life lived for his Savior. Ali will be what you lost in Charlie. He will be a great friend and you will teach each other of the Lord's love."

The encouraging angel stopped talking as they started walking down the streets of gold. Everything was so perfect, so joyful. There were flowers and plants he had never seen before. The music was beyond compare. Every note penetrated Tom's soul and deposited unspeakable joy. The smells were like the sweetest of perfumes. People from everywhere stopped to thank Tom for his obedience.

"How do these people know me?" he asked.

"Everyone here knows you. You are well known and highly esteemed. They talk of your calling and your missions on the earth. That's why you don't need to be famous on the earth. They know you will lay your life down because of your love for the Lord," the angel said.

They stopped at the door of a beautiful house. Tom knew he was supposed to enter. He gazed at the open foyer. He saw pictures on the wall of people who seemed familiar. He heard the loud clatter of someone running down the stairs. As he turned to see who it was, he was being hugged. It was Bill, and he was jumping around like a five year old on Christmas Day.

"Tom, you're here. Yes, Yes, Yes! God is so good." Bill shouted.

Tom stuttered because he didn't know what to say to his friend. "It is so good to see you," he finally got out.

"Can I show you my house?" Bill asked.

"Sure," Tom said as a smile filled his face.

There were flowers and trinkets everywhere. Bill explained: "When I did something for someone in love, they remember it. When they come here to visit me, they bring me a token of their appreciation. Sometimes it's a flower; sometimes it's an item that helps me remember the event. Every time I reached out to someone, even a stranger in kindness, they came here to fill my home. I am so blessed. I never knew such a reward was coming to me. If only everyone knew this, it would change so many lives. God is so gracious. Just think: every little thing we do for others in love is forever recorded and rewarded. People have to know that their labor of love is not in vain.

I have something else to tell you. You know the greatest pain of my life was thinking my son died away from the Lord. I had prayed so many nights for him. I was so tempted to be mad at God when I found out he had been murdered because of a drug deal gone bad. Well, he is here," Bill said.

"What?" Tom asked.

"Yes, a few months before I died, I was in the hospital. The prison guards brought in a prisoner getting cancer treatments like me. It turns out that he was the one who killed my son, but it was because my son had given his life to the Lord. It was so hard to forgive the man, but knowing my son was here gave me the strength to love that man. He received the Lord right before he died. Can you believe that those two are friends now? Heaven is so incredible."

Tom and Bill continued talking until the angel reappeared. "The angel says it's time to go," Bill said as he hugged his friend one last time. "Tom, you were always a son to me. I am so thankful God put you into my life."

"I am so thankful for you," Tom replied. "I don't know when I'll be back again."

"It doesn't matter. I know you'll be back," Bill said as the two parted ways.

The angel smiled and turned, leading the way as Tom walked with him. "I am going to show you what worship is," the angel said. The area they were walking through started to become hazy, like a thick fog. They began walking past saints who were standing and singing. They were all facing forward toward a light. The melodies filled every fiber of Tom's being, joy rising with every step. Tom and the encouraging angel strolled past hundreds, even thousands, of worshippers. Each step only increased the rapture in Tom's soul.

The angel's grin kept growing. After what seemed to be a journey of hours, a new sound joined the melodies. Tom looked to the angel for the answer as to why this sound was here.

"You will see," the angel replied as he started to giggle. After more walking, the sound got louder until they were right next to it. The fog started to lift revealing the most beautiful piano he had ever seen. Whoever was playing was banging out the sweetest praise.

"You might know who is playing the piano," the angel said as Tom strained his eyes. Through the brilliant light, he saw his friend Charlie playing.

"Charlie laid down his life for his Lord and for his friends. He knew this was his calling. This was his worship. It is the greatest worship of all. This is why his song has this level of power. Charlie saw the light on the other side of the fire. The beauty guided him through the pain and into the glory," the angel said.

Tom fell to his knees. "I'm sorry, God. I misjudged Your purposes. I misjudged Your plans. I am so sorry." His heartfelt apology was interrupted by the world's greatest bear hug. It was Charlie. The joy that emanated from him left Tom weak.

"Tom, you're here. I'm so happy. Heaven is so awesome. The Lord is so good. He is so good."

The over-spilling joy created a rapturous laughter in both of them. They laid on the streets of heaven laughing for hours. The angel and hundreds of others joined them in the tickle of the Almighty.

When it seemed as though he could stand no more joy, Tom blinked his eyes and was back with Jennifer in the chariot, laughing together as they headed towards earth. Tom felt something in his pocket, reached for it, and found a large gemstone ring. He knew what he was going to do with it.

He looked at Jennifer and said, "When we get back, I have a question for you."

"I know. And the answer is yes," she replied with a rapturous grin.

Trojol was soon back to his next assignment, his next person, his next dream, his next miracle. The best part of the story is that it has only just begun. Trojol walked into another room as a person slept unaware. Trojol brushed back their hair, pulled out a flask of heavenly oil, and said, "Sweet dreams."

CPSIA information can be obtained at www.ICGtesting.com
Printed in the USA
LVOW070113250413

330803LV00001B/3/P